Anna Seghers
Three Women from Haiti

Translated by Douglas Irving

Foreword by Marike Janzen
"Great, Unknown Men: A Black Man against
Napoleon" by Anna Seghers
Historical Context by Douglas Irving

DIÁLOGOS
DIALOGOSBOOKS.COM

Printed in the U.S.A.
First Printing
10 9 8 7 6 5 4 3 2 1   16 17 18 19 20 21

Book and cover design: Bill Lavender
Interior drawings by Armin Münch, by permission of his widow, Marianne

Library of Congress Control Number: 2019931998
Seghers, Anna
Three Women from Haiti / Anna Seghers;
with Douglas Irving (translator)
and Marike Janzen (foreword)
p. cm.
ISBN: 978-1-944884-63-5 (pbk.)

Other editions:
ISBN: 978-1-944884-64-2 (ebook)

DIALOGOSBOOKS.COM

Translator's Acknowledgements

$\mathcal{T}$hank you to Bill Lavender for his continued interest in publishing Anna Seghers's later work in English translation.

Thank you to Monika Melchert, retired curator of the Anna Seghers Museum at Anna-Seghers-Straße 81, Adlershof, Berlin, for facilitating access to original artwork by Armin Münch, gratefully published here with the kind permission of his widow, Marianne.

Warm thanks to Marike Janzen for her introduction, and her helpful email communications.

Thank you very much to Gill Harvey for invaluable copy-editing.

My thanks to the following three people for reviewing this translation in its draft state: Ernest Schonfield of Glasgow University; Rebecca DeWald of online literary journal, Glasgow Review of Books; Steven Lawrie, Germanist and academic par-excellence of Aberdeen University, also a translator and fiction writer. Steven very sadly died suddenly early in 2017 at the age of 52. This translation is respectfully dedicated to his memory.

Contents

Three Women from Haiti

Foreword by Marike Janzen

Anna Seghers's *Three Women from Haiti* traverses five hundred years of modern history through three spare stories about Haitian women. The tales are set during the fifteenth, early nineteenth, and twentieth centuries, respectively. The female protagonist in each story occupies a central role in resistance movements of her time. In *The Hiding Place*, the indigenous woman named Toaliina avoids capture by the Spaniards conquering the island that Columbus named Hispaniola. *The Key* follows the experience of the slave Claudine, who witnesses a slave insurrection on the French colony of Saint-Domingue from inside a wall niche in which her mistress locks her. After her release, she spends the rest of her life in France safeguarding the memory of anti-slavery revolt and its central leader, Toussaint Louverture. *Separation* takes place in Haiti during the rule of the dictator Jean-Claude Duvalier. The story features Luisa, a working-class woman, who is arrested and beaten by Duvalier's secret police unit, the *Tonton Macoutes*, for her association with a library that anti-Duvalier Communists exiled in France are working to establish in Haiti. Though the island holds different names in the distinct periods the stories cover—Hispaniola, Saint-Domingue, and Haiti—in each case, seemingly unremarkable and often largely silent women act in ways that make clear the stakes of the exploitation they experience, and confront.

In *Three Women from Haiti*, Seghers trains her eye on marginalized people and, for many of her readers, a marginal place. This focus on the seemingly insignificant characterizes her entire *oeuvre*, and serves to question the legitimacy of historical narratives crafted by those in power. Seghers's attention to the experiences of women in Haiti forcefully upends dominant modes of history telling on at least three levels. First, by focusing primarily on events in Haiti, Seghers implicitly challenges the notion that Western Europe should serve as the central point of departure for making sense of modern history. Further, by paying attention to Haitians' acts of resistance against oppression, Seghers suggests that Haiti played a central role in the history of emancipatory movements; this is a role that historians have traditionally granted to European revolutionary movements that grew out of the Enlightenment. Finally, by positing women on the margins as the protagonists in her history of modernity, Seghers rejects the notion that powerful men drive history. Simply put, Seghers's slim volume *Three Women from Haiti* pushes readers to consider peripheral places and people as, in fact, central to global historical development.

Seghers's understanding of Haiti as a fundamental site of emancipatory struggle in modernity grew out of her specific relationship to German politics and letters of the twentieth century. Her exile from fascist Germany in Mexico led Seghers through the Caribbean, where she became aware of the region's historical significance as a space of encounter between Europe, Africa, and the New World. And when Seghers, a committed

Communist author, decided to continue her post-exile career in East Germany, she offered her explorations of revolutionary histories, such as Haiti's, as important perspectives on her new nation's stated project of combating exploitation. Yet the significance of her interest in Haiti extends far beyond a German sphere. Seghers's view of Haiti as a place that could offer crucial lessons for understanding global mechanisms of exploitation and resistance responds to and exists in conversation with anti- and post-colonial intellectual movements of the second half of the twentieth century.

Seghers, who lived from 1900 to 1983, was born into a well-to-do assimilated Jewish family in Mainz, Germany. In 1928, she received the prestigious Kleist Prize for her novella *The Revolt of the Fishermen of St. Barbara* and joined the German Communist Party. The two events mark her emergence as a politically committed writer, an identity she claimed until her death. Yet Seghers's religious background and political affiliation made her a target of the Nazi Party, and she was forced to flee Germany in 1933. Seghers lived in Paris from 1933 until 1940, when Germany occupied France. She found her second exile home in Mexico. Her complicated voyage from Paris to Mexico City required her to sail from Martinique to the Dominican Republic. On that leg of her journey, Seghers took note of two women from Spain conversing in Spanish with black sailors. Even though she couldn't understand much of what they were saying, that moment opened her eyes to, in her words, the "magnitude, the violence of the fallen Spanish colonial power, the breadth of the 'Conquista.'" The fact that "on this spot, the most remote one [she] had reached, a portion of the population spoke Spanish," revealed to Seghers the way that the stories of Europe and the New World were intertwined.[1]

After World War II, Seghers decided to live in East Germany. The work she produced there, during the second half of her life, reflects a sustained interest in Latin America and its relationship to Europe. From the time of her exile in Mexico City until her death, Seghers frequently published fictional texts set in Latin America, as well essays on Latin American writers and revolutionary figures, and book reviews on Latin American literature.[2] One of Seghers's primary goals in producing this work was to teach Germans about non-European history and highlight its significance for their own lives. Her authorial internationalism, then, offered a model for the official solidarity professed by the state, and arguably outreached it.

Haiti regularly figures as a setting for non-fictional and

---

1 — "Vor mir an Deck, wahrscheinlich genau so erschöpft wie ich, lagen zwei spanische Frauen. Sie sprachen spanisch (sic) mit den Negermatrosen. Im Zuhören—ohne daß ich viel verstand—wurde mir plötzlich die Größe, die Gewalt der vergangenen spanischen Kolonialmacht klar, die Breite der 'Conquista,' der einstmaligen spanischen Eroberungen, die der Grund dafür waren, daß hier an dem fernsten Punkt, den ich auf Erden erreicht hatte, ein Teil der Bevölkerung spanisch sprach." Seghers, Anna. *Karibische Geschichten*. Berlin: Aufbau Taschenbuch Verlag, 2000, p. 252

2 — Seghers's fictional works set in Latin America include her short story "Ausflug der toten Mädchen" ("Excursion of the Dead Girls") (1946), *Crisanta: Mexikanische Novelle* (*Crisanta: Mexican Novella*) (1951), *Karibische Geschichten* (*Caribbean Stories*) (1962), "Das wirkliche Blau: Eine Geschichte aus Mexiko" ("The Real Blue: A Story from Mexico") (1967), *Überfahrt, eine Liebesgeschichte* (*Crossing: A Love Story*) (1971). Her essays on Latin American artists and politicians include pieces on Diego Rivera, Tina Modotti, Pablo Neruda, Jorge Amado, Jacques Roumain, and Olga Benario Prestes.

fictional reflections on European-New World connections that Seghers wrote in the late 1940s, the early 1960s, and the late 1970s. When examined within the context of East German political developments in which they were written, it is possible to see Seghers's "Haiti" works as commentary on the German Democratic Republic's development as a state that promised to achieve emancipation from exploitation.

In 1946, immediately after Germany's defeat and occupation by the Allied forces of Great Britain, France, the Soviet Union and the United States of America, Seghers conceived a series of features on Latin American leaders of independence movements in the nineteenth century, *Große Unbekannte* (*Great, Unknown Men*).[3] In addition to essays on the Venezuelan Francisco de Miranda (1750-1816), and the Mexican José María Morelos (1765-1815), Seghers wrote the piece *Ein Neger gegen Napoleon* (*A Black Man against Napoleon*),[4] about the life of Toussaint Louverture (1743-1803) and his fight against slavery in the French colony of Saint-Domingue. Two of these planned essays appeared in the journal *Ost und West* (*East and West*), published with the purpose of bringing together German readers living in the four zones occupied by the different allied powers. Seghers's stated aim in these biographical sketches was to introduce Germans to significant historical figures they had never heard of and broaden their understanding of world history. In the context of post-war, occupied Germany, Seghers's project served two purposes. Her biographies challenged the

---

3 — "Große Unbekannte," *Ost und West: Beiträge zu kulturellen und politischen Fragen der Zeit*, 1, 1947, 7-21

4 — "Ein Neger gegen Napoleon," *Ost und West: Beiträge zu kulturellen und politischen Fragen der Zeit*, 3, 1948, 51-64

racist, nationalist history writing available to Germans under Hitler. Moreover, Seghers's portrayals of men who fought to bring about a new social order inspired Germans to consider non-European histories of revolution and social change when working to rebuild their own nation. This motive held particular relevance in Germany's Soviet-occupied zone, where leaders held up Soviet revolutionary history as the appropriate model for shaping a new, socialist, state. Seghers's portrayal of Toussaint Louverture as a hero was a radical one, as it pushed German readers to consider political models not likely to be promoted by either former or future leaders.

Between the end of the war and 1962, as Stalinist show trials shattered intellectuals' trust in the revolutionary state and each other, Seghers wrote three novellas about eighteenth-century slave uprisings in the Caribbean that were published as the trilogy *Caribbean Stories* (*Karibische Geschichten*). The works, set in Haiti, Guadeloupe, and Jamaica, all focus on Napoleon's decision to reinstate slavery in France's Caribbean territories, variously depicting the way that slaves, *gens de couleurs*, and French emissaries all experienced this move as a betrayal. The trilogy's first novella, *Die Hochzeit von Haiti* (*A Wedding in Haiti*), features Toussaint Louverture's development from coachman of a plantation owner to revolutionary leader, and finally to his demise as Napoleon's prisoner. Instead of approaching Louverture's life as a biography, however, Seghers tells his story in a way that offers insight into the perspectives of people from various social and racial categories whose lives are affected by Louverture's deeds. The ramifications of Louverture's actions affect not only one group of people, but are significant for all;

the work he does can potentially usher in a new world order. The emancipatory impulse Louverture represents is quashed by Napoleon, who lures Louverture to a meeting with false promises of negotiation and takes him prisoner. The question left for readers engaging with the story of slavery's abolition and reinstatement remains: can the revolution's ideals remain alive, even when the state abandons them?

In the late 1970s, a time characterized by artists' disenchantment with the "real existing socialism" that East Germany claimed to have achieved, Seghers again drew on Haiti as the setting for fictional work. The stories in this volume, *Three Women from Haiti*, exist as a pendant to her earlier trilogy on male revolutionary heroes, *Great, Unknown Men*. Rather than offering a creative impetus to a fledgling state, as she had done with *Große Unbekannte*, *Three Women from Haiti* responds to a revolutionary project, the East German state itself, whose emancipatory promise had thus far not been borne out. In these stories, women exist and act as agents within liberatory movements, but not one of them lives to experience the emancipation for which they work. Toaliina remains captive in the cave to which she flees to survive the counter-insurgency, only ultimately managing to escape to her almost-certain death. It is not likely that Claudine will live to see her wish come true, namely, the time when "every slave in the world [will] rise from the dead" (51). Luisa survives her time in prison, but her injuries are so severe that she does not live long after the Duvalier regime has been toppled (an outcome that had not yet occurred when Seghers wrote the story). Is it possible that Seghers, at the end of her life, was using the stories of women in Haiti to consider her own fate as a Communist who would likely not live to see the realization of her revolutionary hopes?

Seghers was one of the most significant writers in East Germany, a state that valued literature as a primary means of shaping revolutionary, socialist thought and for that reason channeled substantial resources to its production. One can assume that Seghers had the East German context in mind when considering the relevance of her subject matter—including her writing on Haiti. And yet Seghers's work on Haiti, in particular *Three Women from Haiti*, holds much broader relevance than as a sorrowful reflection on the status of revolution in what would turn out to be a short-lived state. Instead, Seghers's tales of Haitian women's resistance to oppression that span the modern era must be read as part of an international conversation by major anti-colonial and post-colonial thinkers of the twentieth century. In particular, Seghers's move in *Three Women from Haiti*, to assert erased histories and silenced voices of colonized women as the fulcrum of historical development, rather than one of its effects, resonates with the work of a key theorist of the colonial and post-colonial condition, Gayatri Chakravorty Spivak.

In her groundbreaking essay *Can the Subaltern Speak?*, published in 1988, eight years after *Three Women from Haiti*, Spivak focuses on the mechanisms by which women's voices are silenced when others speak for them—even when those taking on women's causes, including women themselves, are working towards women's liberation. Spivak grounds her discussion in a history of *sati*, or widow self-immolation, in India. In pre-colonial, colonial, and post-colonial contexts, Spivak explains, it was the authorities, not the women themselves, who interpreted the practice as either positive or problematic. Women's own grounds for participation in *sati*, which, of course, cannot be verified after the fact, never figured in either the justification or condemnation of the act. Spivak's difficult conclusion is that the subaltern, those subject to authority, cannot speak because they cannot be heard. The voiceless are not audible to those who have the agency to represent, to speak for, the voiceless. As a result, it behooves those who work against exploitation, including those leftist intellectuals making pronouncements about the condition of people in the "third world" to whom Spivak addresses her essay, to understand this phenomenon.

At the same time that Spivak was theorizing exploited women's ability to act as historical agents in transforming injustice, Seghers took on the same question in a way that resonates with Spivak—albeit in the context of Haiti. Spivak concerns herself with the way that women's voices exist at the center of struggles against exploitation, but do not figure in official historical accounts of those events. In a parallel fashion, Seghers's depiction of women in Haiti highlights how women exist at the center of resistance movements, yet their bodies are similarly immobilized and silenced. Toaliina is confined to a cave in *The Hiding Place*, Claudine is imprisoned by a mistress in *The Key*, and Luisa is rendered almost mute by the beatings she receives in prison in *Separation*. Just as Spivak critiques those who speak for the oppressed and thereby silence them,

Seghers's stories identify a consistent blind spot at the heart of emancipatory movements: silent and trapped women.

By thus highlighting women's unheard voices in the key historical moments of modernity—Europeans' encounter with the New World, slavery, and post-colonialism—Seghers suggests that these silences constitute the historical narrative. Yet the potential fatalism of this perspective is negated by the dialectical relationship structuring each story: redemption, even if just a glimmer of it, accompanies women's silencing. The final scene of *The Hiding Place* portrays Toaliina after the storm waves have washed away her cave: she is clinging to rocks with all the strength she has left and realizes that "her escape had succeeded" (34). Seghers describes what are likely Toaliina's final moments not as imminent death, but in terms of her consciousness that her life was shaped by resistance. The end of *The Key* focuses on Claudine at the funeral of her husband, Amédée, who wears the key he used to free her from her mistress's closet around his neck. Claudine rejects suggestions that she should now wear it. The key stands for more than her personal rescue: it exists as a reminder of a larger struggle for abolition. The work's final story, like the first two, ends with a woman's silencing, as Luisa does not survive for long after her prison rescue. The "fine" and very public "funeral procession" held for her seems to discount the secret work she undertook to help the revolution, work that eventually led to her death. And yet those who witness it also receive inspiration from her story.

The dialectical pairing Seghers presents between, on the one hand, silenced women, and, on the other hand, redemption, does not translate to the lesson that oppressed women must be martyrs. There is barely an audience either for Toaliina's suffering in the cave or Claudine's shouts for help from the plantation-house wall prison. Those who honor Luisa do so without necessarily understanding that she did not make her sacrifices for the honors that she might receive. Yet these women are not victims. Instead, they are agents in the way they recognize the consequences of their actions. A central point Seghers wants to make by telling about the fate of women in Haiti across the span of five centuries is that we cannot grasp the depth of world history without acknowledging its unrecognized actors.

After the end of the Cold War, readers in a newly reunited Germany had little interest in East German authors who had not been outspoken dissidents in the GDR. Though Seghers did issue criticism of East Germany, she only did so either "between the lines" of her texts or behind the scenes. Nevertheless, in the context of post-reunification Germany, Seghers was seen as having bought into state dogma, thus compromising her authenticity as an artist. This understanding of Seghers primarily in relation to the East German state may explain why there has been very little attention paid to her final, slim volume, let alone recognition for the significance of her reflections on Haitian history.

And yet, Seghers's assertion of Haiti as being at the center, and not the margin, of the world, is revolutionary. She refutes, implicitly, the racism that, according to Haitian scholar

Michel-Rolph Trouillot, historically made black agency in Haiti "unthinkable."[5] This racism, tragically, continues to shape attitudes toward the country.

Despite making an argument for a reconceptualization of world history, the stories in *Three Women from Haiti* are not bombastic, but quiet. One has to pay careful attention to hear their message. They are telling us that, in order to understand history, one must look to what is not immediately visible and listen for the silent voices.

5 — Michel-Rolph Trouillot, *Silencing the Past: Power and the Production of History*, Boston: Beacon Press, 1995, 73.

It may be that some of the characters from the works of Anna Seghers rank among the last revolutionaries in German literature.... What would the twentieth century be without them?

—Christa Wolf, "Gesichter der Anna Seghers," in *Anna Seghers. Eine Biographie in Bildern*, ed. by Frank Wagner et al. (Berlin: Aufbau Verlag, 1994), pp. 6-9 (p. 9)

Anna Seghers
Three Women from Haiti

The Hiding Place

The Key

Separation

Précis from the original Aufbau-Verlag edition

*E*ver since Anna Seghers became acquainted with the Dominican part of Hispaniola under the Trujillo dictatorship during her flight from Europe to Mexico, the turbulent history of this Caribbean island preoccupied her. After returning to Germany, between 1948 and 1962 she wrote her first trilogy, *Caribbean Stories*, three of her best stories (*A Wedding in Haiti*; *The Reinstatement of Slavery in Guadeloupe*; *The Light on the Gallows: a Caribbean Tale from the Time of the French Revolution*).

Almost two decades later, she takes up the theme again in this, her last book. In this set of stories about three women who lived in Haiti at different times, we are presented with three different eras through the fates of Toaliina, Claudine and Luisa, characterized by persecution, escape and extreme peril: the conquering of the island by Columbus; the revolt of black slaves under Toussaint Louverture; and the military dictatorships of Papa and Bébé Doc.

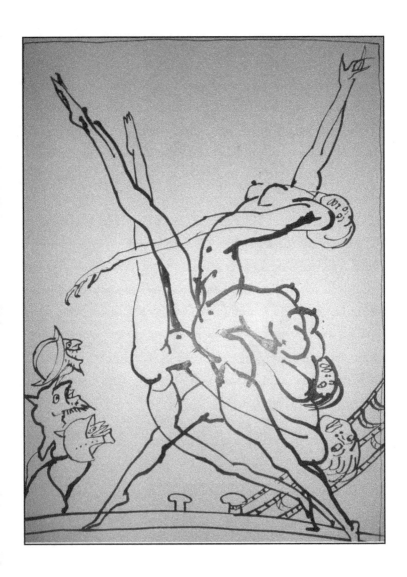

The Hiding Place

The third time Columbus sailed from Haiti to Spain to report to the queen, his ships were not freshly laden with gold, as had been hoped, but with reddish- and light-colored timber unknown in Europe, with seeds and fruit, bales of cloth.

Above all, Columbus had fulfilled the queen's express wish: he was bringing her twelve very young girls, whom he had hailed in his reports as heavenly in grace and beauty.

Queen Isabella intended to raise these girls at the Spanish court and there have them serve, to the wonderment of her guests. The most graceful ones were destined as gifts for several noblemen who had been of outstanding service to the crown.

The girls flashed past each other like flying fish as they danced under the evening sun on the deck of the admiral ship. The loveliest among them had been given the name Toaliina by locals, and the name had stuck. Toaliina's companions clustered around her. They displayed themselves to the islanders who were following the ships' departure from the coast, near to the landing stage guarded by the Spaniards. On deck, crew members admired the dancers from a distance. They were forbidden to touch any of the girls, however fleetingly.

The anchors were raised. With a deep breath the coastline began to fade from view.

Toaliina made a bird-call then swung herself over the railing. Instantly every girl dived after her. With steady strokes they made for the point on the shore they had moments ago left. From there, individual cries carried across the water, perhaps to warn or to encourage.

A very agile ship's boy dived after Toaliina. Lighting fast she turned and bit his hand. Meanwhile several boats were lowered. The girls formed a chain, and Toaliina swam at its head. The seamen gave chase, swimming or rowing.

Had they struck the girls or—perish the thought—shot at them, it would not have been possible to parade them before the Spanish court as creatures of heavenly grace.

Toaliina changed course. Two of her companions had been captured while still at sea; these girls had kept straight for shore. Others had been seized by guards as they arrived. The onlookers' faces clouded over. A short time ago they had smiled as the ships departed; now they seemed to grasp what was at stake. The recaptured girls were locked in dark cabins.

On board the ship they puzzled as to why the girls had attempted to escape. "They have no idea what Spain is." — "And what it would mean for them to serve at the Spanish royal court." Two friends commented that the admiral's guest yesterday had been a brother of the chief. They said that, when he brought the parting gifts, he had exchanged a quiet word with Toaliina and signaled to her with his hand.

Toaliina did not swim for shore. She hid in some floating weed, then came ashore a good distance from the landing stage. With swift, sure steps she strode toward a hollow. There she stood still and peered into a huge tree crown that had been torn from its trunk, either intentionally or by a storm. The crown had re-rooted. From the branches crawled an old woman. She withdrew again after ensuring that Toaliina followed unhesitatingly behind. The old woman said nothing; she did not beckon. She merely raised her index finger against the rock face to which fresh branches clung.

Following the old woman, Toaliina scrambled between the rocks. Only the occasional shaft of light penetrated the myriad passages and caves. Toaliina thought then of the words the Haitian had hissed to her when he brought the gifts for the Spanish court onto the admiral ship. Clearly this brother of the chief had not come aboard solely on account of the parting gifts, but to offer Toaliina one or two words of counsel. Unlike his brother he had, along with many islanders, mistrusted the Spaniards from the outset. He had signaled to Toaliina: "For as long as you live, you will only be safe with that woman, the mother of my friend."

Toaliina had not thought about these words, and neither did she think now about what it could mean: *for as long as you live.*

The old woman made her way through the rock face as easily and sure-footedly as though there were a path. Toaliina crawled after her. They came to a halt in a cave. Its walls were bare; on ledges here and there stood an array of utensils. On the ground lay a few blankets. These were trampled and worn, but judging by their color and texture, such blankets could readily have been added to the gifts bound for Spain. Already Toaliina craved air and the sound of the sea.

The old lady ground a paste from bulbs and roots. Footsteps were heard from a rear entrance. "Tshanangi! My son!"

exclaimed the woman. And she ground with gleeful gusto. Toaliina beamed at the sight of the newcomer, he at the sight of her.

Tshanangi reported that three girls had been seized no sooner had they reached shore. He said that the Spaniards had hunted down two others and found their lodgings. The girls were brutally beaten. They were locked up. Their huts were burned down.

"Brutally beaten! Burned down!" cried Toaliina.

"I assure you," said the young Haitian, as he ran his lips tenderly along Toaliina's arm.

"The chief would have us believe," he continued, "that the gods sent these strangers to us, but from the beginning his brother took them to be distant island dwellers who sailed here for booty. The truth has duly emerged. We are no longer united on this island."

"When you come to us again, take another route," Tshanangi's mother told him. "Through the forest. Only we know of this entrance. Toaliina mustn't go out at all. Her hair is black, but with golden patches. She's easily recognized from afar."

Toaliina was intoxicated by her love for Tshanangi. She no longer understood time. She understood nothing of the time between two embraces; nothing of the time between his leaving and his returning.

She bore a son. On that day, Tshanangi came later than ever. Tied around his neck he wore a strange coin threaded on a string. "Whoever doesn't wear a coin on a string will be arrested," he explained. "It's the mark of the gold tribute. It's tied around the neck of everyone who pays up. I don't know whether this admiral is good or bad. His men grow unruly when his back is turned, like now. He cannot rein them in from afar. Any of us who doesn't hand over his gold tribute is sent to the mine. There he must dig from the earth what he failed to freely hand over."

Another time Tshanangi said, "The admiral has returned with his friend. He wasn't happy about how events have been unfolding here. These Spaniards are brazen and cruel. You, Toaliina, take not one step away from here."

She thought again—only now anxiously—of the words the chief's brother had uttered to her on the ship: *"For as long as you live, you will be safe in that place with the mother of my friend."*

Toaliina's heart ached for the sea. One evening Tshanangi carried their newborn child through the rear entrance to the shore. When it lay in her arms again, Toaliina sucked in the salt smell.

The old woman died. Being alone was bitter.

After much waiting—and by now Toaliina understood what waiting was—instead of Tshanangi came his best friend. "Tshanangi described the way to you, in detail," he said. "He ended up in the gold mine after all. It's easier for me to live here with you rather than outside, under threat from the Spaniards."

In Cádiz, Columbus was not received quite as warmly as on his last return. He was informed that, in his stead, various new commanders-in-chief of newly discovered countries and islands had been appointed. In Haiti, in his absence, the fortress of La Navidad had been destroyed; there too a new governor had been appointed in Columbus's stead.

Because of his insubordination, the brother of the old chief (who had thought of gifts for the Spanish court before Columbus's last departure) was stripped of all honor. Along with many Haitians he was forced into hiding in mountains to the west of the island. From the start, they had taken the Spanish newcomers to be not gods but greedy, sanctimonious invaders. Now it was clear who was against whom. On a high pass, the Haitians clashed with the Spaniards. The Spaniards fought with superior weapons. The defeated Haitians were turned into slaves.

All this Toaliina was told by Tshanangi's friend. He stayed hidden in the cave. He slipped out as little as possible by a side path, only to fetch fruit and water. Toaliina learned to prepare him delicious meals, as Tshanangi's mother had done. She lived with this friend, not as happy as before, but without hardship. She bore him two children.

Meanwhile, in Spain, Queen Isabella had asked of the clergy and high church officials whether trading and selling slaves were permissible. After thorough investigation the answer was, "Yes; perfectly permissible, even in the Holy Scriptures."

The loveliest and nimblest of the girls who had once escaped with Toaliina but were recaptured served initially at court and in the houses of noblemen. Once the men had had their fill of them, these girls ended up at the slave markets. Even so, it is said that some remained the mistresses and wives of noble lords.

After he returned to Haiti, Columbus in his fever for

discovery embarked on many fresh voyages. Nothing could dissuade him from viewing the islands and coastlines to which he ventured as parts of India—the Orinoco, whose delta he invaded, he took to be one of the great Indian waterways.

The Spanish court was certainly excited by these new discoveries, but far more so by events in their own country. At court, one wedding followed another; the youngest princess, sister of the heir to the Spanish throne, married the sovereign lord of the Netherlands.

*T*shanangi, Toaliina's first husband, had long since fled the mine. He reached a mountain range in the west controlled by a Chief Bujarda, who at no time had taken the strange newcomers to be gods; it had become increasingly clear to him and his supporters that nasty, greedy, deceitful people were plundering their island on regular booty raids. Before long, Tshanangi ranked among Bujarda's best guards and companions-in-arms. When Tshanangi was carried back into the mountain retreat, fatally wounded following a Spanish attack, in his fever it seemed to him he lay in the cave that had long been his shelter; the woman nursing him seemed lovelier than any other. The sight of her overwhelmed him with happiness. Tshanangi forgot his wounds as he searched for her name. Suddenly wide awake, he cried, "Toaliina!" With this memory, he held death at bay for a time.

The Haitian who was now Toaliina's husband, upon leaving the cave to look for food, made an all-too-rash, all-too-naïve wrong turn. Guards challenged him.

"Where are you from? What's your master's name?" They bombarded him with questions.

"Master of the mountains in the west," he replied.

These mountains were considered impregnable. To the question as to whom, in that case, he intended to visit, he replied: any who would listen to him.

They tied him up and whipped him; under relentless interrogation they rubbed salt into his bleeding lacerations. He laughed, and was willing to be beaten to death. Never would he reveal the place where Toaliina was hiding, which had become a refuge for many a victim of persecution.

With time, no one looked for her hiding place any longer. There were probably one or two people who surmised that she was hiding somewhere in the mountains; after all, she could not have vanished like a ghost after reaching land.

$\mathcal{T}$he heir to the Spanish throne, Juan (who had married a daughter from the Netherlands royal family), died suddenly. A funeral ceremony followed the wedding. In the making was the Spanish-Netherlands alliance that would tear Europe asunder for another hundred years.

Perhaps from time to time someone slipped into Toaliina's hiding place, someone in mortal danger to whom knowledge of this refuge had been entrusted. Perhaps now and then one man said to another, "That'll be where the woman lives who many years ago was to be sold to Spain and dived from the admiral ship and swam back and hid here on the coast."

Thus Toaliina learned of her own past, which she had all but forgotten, except for the roar of the waves.

One day as she lay in her cave a violent storm broke. The sea tore away sections of coastline. Trees were uprooted. The cave walls collapsed. Toaliina crawled through the rear entrance, which was already partially blocked. She clung to some rock to catch her breath. Soon her face was bitten raw by the salt air. *Where are my children? In the mine? In chains? In prison? At sea?* At any moment the surge might sweep her away. She clawed at a fragment of rock with the last of her strength. For all the danger, she sensed coming to her aid the sea she had known since childhood.

She knew her escape had succeeded.

The Key

$\mathcal{T}$he cast-iron drum that had once roasted chestnuts in Paris had cooled. There were no chestnuts here. So at lunchtime the black woman, Claudine, roasted corn, hazelnuts, rosehips and other fruit. Laborers building the great road in the Jura Mountains stopped to buy a handful of what Claudine rustled up. Amédée then laid his wife's scarf over the cooled drum. From his pocket he drew a wine bottle and a hunk of bread which he shared with her. A few people going to Pontarlier or some other village lingered a moment to watch their meager meal. To them everything seemed strange: the drum for roasting corn; the black couple's meal, eaten quickly and mannerly, not greedily, despite their hunger. Mulling it over as they went on their way, the passers-by said:

"He has a cross on a string around his neck."

"That was no cross. It was a key."

"A key?"

"Go closer, then you'll see: a key!"

With his last mouthful, Amédée jumped up to follow his work squad. He had taken the lunch break of his own volition. His foreman had brought over people from Haiti; he had taken on some of them back in Paris and made up the rest of the squad here, from the surrounding area. The contractor in Paris had undertaken to lay the road through the mountains on behalf of the state.

On the ship that brought him to France, Amédée had learned of the latest event to shake the world: Napoleon's coup of 18 Brumaire.

Bonaparte was finally in power. He could not abide black rule in Haiti. He detested black people. He particularly loathed Toussaint, who held power in Haiti and used it wisely. He sent forth warships. The island was shot to smithereens, its farms and forests burned down. Toussaint, leader of the black forces, was tricked into being taken prisoner and was removed to a fortress in the Jura Mountains.

When Amédée learned of these events, he was seized by the fear that Toussaint, whom he loved above all people—it was perhaps only by dint of Toussaint's actions that Amédée had fully understood what it meant to love a person—might come to harm. He managed to find work on the road-building in the Jura. Here, he had the fortress where Toussaint was imprisoned constantly in sight. It felt to Amédée as though Toussaint in his cell knew that one of his most faithful followers was keeping continual watch on his window.

Not all the French soldiers who guarded the fortress or performed a duty there were of one mind—despite the fact that Bonaparte believed everyone should approve of his every command. Amédée discovered a sentry, Jean Violet, who, once they trusted each other, relayed to him everything concerning Toussaint during their brief but regular meetings. And this Violet made no secret of the fact that he likewise considered Toussaint a mighty man who was maltreated because he was feared.

For all Amédée's inextinguishable love, all he now had was this brief glimpse during his break of the fortress window behind which Toussaint likely lived. Which was why he often took a detour on his way to work, and, so that his companions didn't grumble, he brought them corn, rosehips and other things that his wife, Claudine, knew how to prepare.

Amédée did not know, and neither did Jean Violet suspect, that the light in Toussaint's cell was flickering not as a signal to a man in the work squad who was loyal to him, but because at that moment his cell was being ransacked. Amédée believed his beloved Toussaint must have sensed his presence and recognized him.

In an empty farmstead on the road that was being built, quarters had been set up for the foreman, and the cellar was crammed full of laborers. Claudine also slept here, and sometimes her friend Sophie, pressed up against her. Sophie, also a black woman, had accepted the position with her husband in Martinique. Snuggled together for warmth, the two women told each other of their experiences in recent years. Because their tales told of danger and drama, they stayed awake despite their exhaustion.

While Amédée gazed up as long as he could at the fortress—from the road it looked like a rocky promontory—his wife, Claudine, lay pressed against Sophie and told her about her former life as a slave in Haiti.

"Just before the great banquet that the Evremonts gave every year, a vase fell from my hand. My mistress yelled that the vase had been extremely valuable, that it would have cost

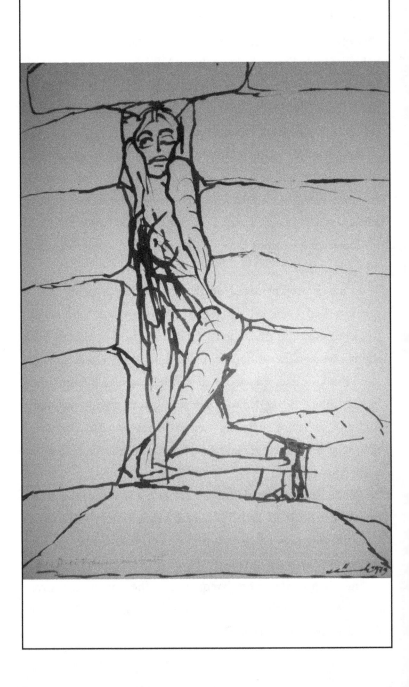

three times as much as me at market. As punishment she had me locked in a tiny cell cut into the wall, which could be seen from the banqueting table. 'If you get bored,' said the wicked woman, 'you can watch the guests.'

"My mistress used to enjoy thinking up such punishments. I was crammed into this niche in the wall. The bars were pushed shut. The housekeeper—although a black like me, she stood in good favor—locked me in and put the key on her necklace. I could barely move a muscle in that niche. I writhed and I groaned. At first the table guests stared, some curious, some perhaps even sympathetic. Now, Sophie, you should know, all sorts of things had already happened that week on the neighboring estates, things I didn't really understand anything about here on my estate, things I didn't ever think possible.

"The new French commissioner had landed. His task was to expropriate the estates and give the people power over the estate owners. He'd failed to find support among blacks and mulattoes—just blinkered, frightened people. In the end he allied himself to Toussaint, who knew how to ignite opposition. On a coffee plantation owned by Count Monrois, not far from the Evremonts, on the morning of the same day they held the banquet on our estate and locked me in my wall prison, not one African turned up for work. Deputies of the commissioner had arranged it so. These deputies laughed at the ensuing violence. And suddenly—but I only heard all this later—two of Count Monrois's coaches pulled up in front of the Evremonts' gate; someone came tearing toward the banquet table—not a black, some spruced-up white, dressed for dinner like our guests—and rushed frantically into the banqueting hall. No one was watching my wall prison any more. Even though my ribs were getting crushed, I couldn't take my eyes off what was suddenly unfolding. Eventually Countess Evremont stood up with a bewildered look; the count stood up, and a man sitting next to them; other guests surrounded the newcomer; finally, everyone stampeded out of the hall in panic. The vases and plates that were broken in the process must have had a value greater than twenty girls like me! The guests piled into the coaches that had been obtained. When these were full, the remaining whites climbed onto some carts that had been harnessed. I think there was just one driving force: away from the estate, down to the coast. Of course, I only learned all this later; I could only confirm what I saw from my barred niche. Sophie, you must believe me, my amazement and exhilaration far outweighed my desperation. Some from the Monrois estate came to ours. There was a smell of burning... I've already told you so much. Do you want to sleep now?"

"Yes, I should sleep. I too witnessed it all. Only I wasn't shut in a wall prison. But how you got out of there—I have to hear that."

"I shook the bars like mad. I thought every bone in my body would break, so hard did I shake, that I might be freed and out with the others. Our blacks did not hear me. They burst into the banqueting hall. They shouted, they rampaged; here and there a flame gobbled up a tablecloth or a curtain. The crockery on the banqueting table had long since been smashed to bits. 'Open up!' I screamed. 'Let me out!' But in their frenzy, our slaves surged past the wall, slashing, tearing, torching everything. No doubt that horrid woman with the bunch of keys who locked me in had already escaped to the harbor in fear of her life."

Sophie no longer felt like sleeping; she was listening intently.

"All our blacks charged, yelling, through the farmhouse. None paid heed to me, little old me. I rattled my bars, I shouted, I screamed, but they, who were in the very act of liberating every black on the island, didn't notice me at all.

"Suddenly, after what seemed like an eternity, one man stopped. He braced himself against the onrushing tide of people; he was big and strong. He bent down to me, said, 'Keep calm. You'll soon be free.' But he was unable to break open the lock with his first attempt. 'Bring the key here!' he boomed.

"I cannot say if my guard—that horrid woman with all the keys jangling round her neck—was already up and away with the whites; I cannot say where my people caught her, or whether they beat her to death. Anyway, they brought my rescuer—Amédée was his name, just like his master—the key to my prison. In a trice I was free. My limbs creaked. When they carried me out of the farmhouse, how happy the air made me! I couldn't thank my rescuer—Amédée was already miles away by then.

"At first, most moved into their masters' former residences. I still remember well when the first ship full of coffee we had picked and ground sailed for France. They said that the French Revolution had liberated us; who that was, what that was, we didn't yet understand at the time. I took the Revolution to be a great big woman around whom we danced, singing.

"They said that one of our number—he had been coachman at a manor house; Toussaint was his name—rode at the head of an army of blacks from one estate to the next. I cheered with the others when this man rode past, even though I didn't quite know why.

"Stay awake, Sophie, a little longer. This next part's important. A great many of us—I was among them—went into the mountains. They said that there, you could see this Toussaint up close; that presently he would address us all. We waited. But before he appeared, my gaze fell upon a black I thought I recognized. A big, strong man. He had a key on a necklace hanging on his chest. I cried out; I pushed my way through the crowds. He recognized me too—it was Amédée, who'd obtained the key and freed me. It was he who spoke first. In his booming voice he told the story of how I was nearly left locked in my wall prison on the Evremont estate while the entire country was liberating itself.

"Suddenly Toussaint arrived, but he stayed back and listened to Amédée. Then he went right up to him. For a moment he held the key hanging on Amédée's chest and regarded it; he stroked my hair—he, Toussaint, amid this throng of people who had waited for him. To this day I can still feel his hand brush my hair. And when I look up at his window in Fort de Joux, where he's imprisoned, I feel the sensation of his hand more strongly than ever."

*T*he winter drew to an end. The people who had built the road through the Jura Mountains were exhausted.

On an April evening, Amédée came later than usual to the cellar quarters, and did not greet Claudine. Silently he lay

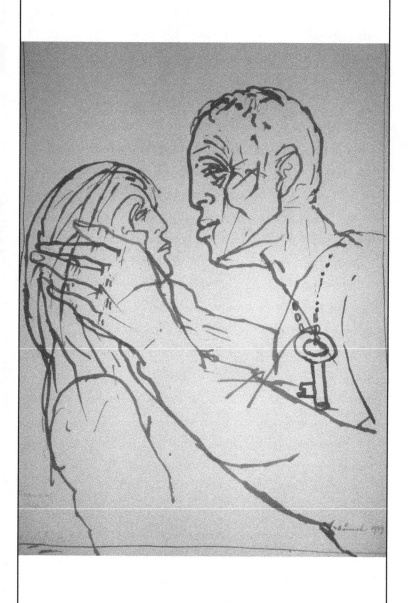

down beside her. His wife had been expecting him. She leaned on her elbows and watched him in surprise. He was breathing hard. She sensed that something was wrong. Amédée could no longer contain himself. Silently he sobbed; repeatedly he gasped for breath; from his chest came a groan.

"You're disturbing our sleep," someone growled.

Amédée crouched close to Claudine. "Toussaint is dead," he said in a hushed voice. "When a guard took him his breakfast this morning, the plate fell from his hand. Toussaint lay slumped in his chair. The commanding officer spread the news at once—such is the fear these people still have of him, even though he lay dead on his chair before their eyes. The parish priest has had to bury him. Toussaint must have been ill here in the bitter cold from the outset. He couldn't bear the icy wind from the moment he came to this harsh corner of the world and was dragged from pillar to post and imprisoned here. You know what a blow it was for me when I learned from Jean that Toussaint was worsening by the day in these mountains. Jean's respect for our Toussaint grew the more ill he became. Not for one moment did the commanding officer suspect that my friend Jean wasn't alone in his respect, his outrage, his sympathy. Be that as it may, Toussaint is dead."

Amédée sobbed silently. Claudine wiped his face. She was crying herself.

Three nights later, Claudine was waiting anxiously for her husband, as she did every evening. She no longer told stories. Probably Sophie was glad to get to sleep early. On the fourth evening, Amédée came late. "The commanding officer," he told Claudine, "who carries out to the letter all that the Paris ministers order, wants to draw a veil over what a man Toussaint was. Against his own will, he has had to find a decent burial site for Toussaint among the veterans' graves." For a moment he was silent. Claudine thought he had fallen asleep. But briefly he spoke again. "If I die before you, do not take the key from me; leave it around my neck."

"Why do you speak of death? Granted, life is hard. But we'll both live a little longer yet. After all, we're not the only ones—you said so yourself—who are suffering on account of Toussaint's death; this Jean, who told you everything, understands well what a man he was."

"He's not the only one at the fort, nor is he the only one in France; don't forget—the Jacobins didn't all die when Bonaparte rose to power."

Amédée, on his lowly bed, was not alone in weeping. In the town of Joux, in many villages in the Jura Mountains, rumors circulated about Toussaint's death. People who had hardly heard of Toussaint when he was alive spoke of him in the taverns and in their homes. "He was feared in chains," Jean said to Amédée. "He remains so in the grave as well."

In Paris, members of a society called the Friends of the Blacks were distraught about Toussaint's death. It spurred them to meet again, although their society was on the police list of suspicious organizations. And in Bordeaux, where the society also had a branch, they started to collect money for a memorial. Toussaint's son, who in those days lived in Bordeaux, had been raised in France; at the time, his father had thought that his son would receive an education and a good upbringing in this country.

Even in the slave quarters of the great American farms, people were heartbroken to hear of Toussaint's death. The news had spread everywhere that black people contemplated their fate.

Just as Amédée had once so fervently wished to move near to the fortress where Toussaint lived and ultimately died, now his sole wish was to visit the grave of the man to whom his heart was devoted.

Suddenly from the city of Bordeaux came an offer to house the dead man in the municipal cemetery. It was Toussaint's son who had purchased the burial plot. The Society of the Friends of the Blacks had recently been outlawed by the police, and its Paris branch had been disbanded; the society no longer received protection or funding, but it maintained its support in small groups here and there. This son of Toussaint sponsored one such support group in Bordeaux.

Amédée and Claudine had for a long time led a miserable existence in the Jura. Even though the road-building had come to an end in this part of the mountains and another group of workers had moved into the old farmstead, Amédée and Claudine were still allowed their bed at night because on cold nights Amédée used his little chestnut stove for heating in exchange for accommodation. Claudine also saw to the preparation of different drinks from tree bark and dried fruit.

It did her husband good to visit Toussaint's grave regularly at Fort de Joux. When he suddenly learned that the dead man was to be removed to a distant city, Amédée was determined to follow him. His determination knew no bounds. When he told Claudine of his resolve, she was ready at once for the difficult

journey; the memory of those terrible hours in the wall prison many years ago had never left her, any less than her gratitude towards Amédée.

Exhausted and starving, the two eventually arrived in Bordeaux. A graveyard attendant showed them the way to Toussaint's grave. In this city they at last found chestnuts again, and fed themselves by means of the little stove which they had somehow managed to carry with them—one more reason for Claudine to approve of her husband's determination.

After about a week, a city local who had observed their graveyard visits addressed them there. Amédée told the man all they had lived through, and showed him the key, and said, "Yes, this is the woman here." Claudine was old and shrunken by now.

The local man took them both to like-minded friends. They were given work and lodgings.

This group, a remnant of the Society of the Friends of the Blacks, invited them regularly, albeit with great caution. Then Amédée would recount his tale, and Claudine would timidly and shyly answer this question and that.

With Napoleon having been crowned emperor and most countries in Europe undergoing transformation, people had more on their minds than erecting a monument in a Bordeaux cemetery. Though the Paris branch of the Society of the Friends of the Blacks had long since been disbanded, in Bordeaux and in other cities one or two groups still gathered. They said that, for all Napoleon's victories, in Haiti he had met with defeat;

they perceived that he was not unconquerable, as had appeared the case. Perhaps this small network of friends were the only ones to regard Napoleon's invasion of Russia as futile.

Before his death, Amédée witnessed Napoleon's army perish in Berezina. To many people this defeat seemed incomprehensible. Amédée compared it to his defeat on Haiti, when French warships had been unable to capture the island.

Amédée's final wish was to be buried near Toussaint. Before the burial, the friends took the key from his chest and asked Claudine to wear it from then on. They had bought a silver necklace. They told her the key with which her husband had opened her wall prison was to hang on it. They said she was to wear it always—on holidays, at work.

Claudine, whom they knew as shy and timid, angrily interrupted them. "No—Amédée shall wear it until every slave in the world rises from the dead."

They obeyed her wish, and Amédée was buried with the key on his chest. At his funeral, those who cast a handful of sand into the grave felt united with the dead man.

Separation

$\mathcal{L}$uisa waited on the jetty. From here you could sail with the small steamboat to the island opposite. Then she had only a half-hour walk to Santa Dolores School. By a series of happy coincidences, but chiefly due to her friend Sophia's ingenuity, the school was already in its fifth year, attended by a growing number of children, mostly those of wealthy traders who had their shops by the quay and their residences by the sea.

As soon as the boat left the jetty the passengers congregated on deck. They scarcely glanced at the open water. The broad bay bustled with fishing boats. Some passengers offered their verdict on the likely successes of the fishermen. Whoever struck lucky would sell his fresh catch straightaway at market, if it were not already reserved by one or two families or restaurants. The passengers followed with particular interest the boats that called at one island after the other; most of these islands had been cleared and many were populated, belonging to wealthy owners. There were also islets with space for just one or two huts; twice a year these dwellings were swept away when the wind blew fiercely from the north-west. The passengers knew all the owners; their conversations grew lively.

Most had not spotted a solitary ship out to sea, a dot that eventually detached itself from other dots. Only Luisa had unwaveringly kept this dot in sight since their departure. Near her a passenger commented casually, "That one sails to Mexico. Once a month. Whoever wants to go to the USA sails from there to Florida." No specific details were mentioned. It had not occurred to anyone that this journey to Florida via Mexico could be the first stage of a journey to Cuba.

As the ship suddenly disappeared over the horizon, Luisa's face was wet with tears. She had not realized that her crying had intensified. She could not help herself; her heart was fit to break. An old woman whom Luisa had not noticed came up to her and asked, "Do you need anything, my child?"

"No, thank you," replied Luisa, who knew how to compose herself swiftly. "It's just that I had to say goodbye to my mother. She's very ill."

The old woman made to comfort her, but as the boat docked Luisa said a quick goodbye; she wanted to make her way to Santa Dolores School alone.

When Luisa arrived, Sophia was called from class with the news that her friend had suddenly appeared. She was surprised, because Luisa was employed by the storekeeper Lopez, who always kept her on a tight rein. She was startled at the sight of Luisa's face: a stark, frozen beauty she hadn't seen before.

Without a word of greeting, Luisa blurted, "Cristobal's gone with Filipe. Both got visas. I watched their ship disappear. How can I describe it? The earth is round, and suddenly their ship was gone. Perhaps I'll never see him again." Once more, tears streamed down her face. She could not contain herself.

Sophia was so taken aback by this tearful outburst that she snapped, "Be glad he got away in time," and went back to her class.

Luisa thought: *I'll never see him again.* He *was the tiny dot that disappeared three hours ago. I'm sure if they'd searched for him here and caught him, then he'd have been killed. My heart would have broken. Now, though, it's breaking without end...*

A few weeks later Luisa was sitting with Sophia on San Anton quay.

All around them were the sounds of guitars playing, singing, shouting. Luisa stared at the horizon as though today she could bring back the ship that had disappeared before her eyes: Cristobal would arrive here at San Anton quay, he would embrace her, they would go laughing into town. As if reading her thoughts, the teacher said, "You'll never see him again. Even if you do see him somewhere, you must pretend you haven't."

Suddenly Luisa heard, just nearby, Cristobal's favorite song: "You, Haiti, Daughter of Columbus and the Sea."

"You've never heard this song," Sophia said, "neither now nor before. Yes, he arrived in Cuba. That I heard. He's launched himself into his work. He reckons on returning after two years' study to teach what he has learned."

After two months *he'll realize he's made a mistake*, thought Luisa. *He'll feel that he belongs here, to me and to us. He was probably already thinking these thoughts as I watched him disappear. And already, he'll be regretting letting himself be talked into going away. We'll see each other again soon...*

$\mathcal{T}$he following year, Luisa was sitting with her old school friend, Ana, in the new café opposite the African museum. She was endeavoring to read the notes Ana had written on a napkin. Ana was about to sit an exam. Luisa's family had not raised enough money for music school, only for a course at the business college. Luisa was hardworking, conscientious, reliable. Lopez, for whom she worked, needed reliable employees. You would never catch Luisa going out to enjoy herself. Even before, she had only ever met her boyfriend Cristobal at out-of-the-way places.

All at once in this new café, someone started humming a song: "You, Haiti, Daughter of Columbus and the Sea."

Quickly Luisa scribbled the song notes on the edge of her own napkin and placed her glass of iced coffee on top of it. She was trembling to the core; she dared not turn around. Looking to Ana, she tried to indicate to her which table to place her glass and napkin on.

Suddenly black men in dark glasses stormed into the café, the state police that everyone feared above all. Among Haitians they were called Vodou Devils. Papa Doc had deployed them first; they remained loyal to his son, Bébé Doc. Luisa heard blows, glasses shattering. She heard a rasping voice: "Don't think you all can meet your sweethearts where and when it suits you."

They dragged past a young man from the next table. Despite her terror, Luisa saw that he was not a local. She tore up the scrap of napkin with the notes on.

The waiter, Juan, who had gold buttons sewn on his white jacket, came over to her table. "Please will you also pay for our friend? He left before his companion was arrested."

Luisa stared at him, wide-eyed. Her school friend had

already left the café with the remaining customers. But before long, new clients who had noticed nothing of the incident occupied the empty seats. Luisa paid the small amount. As she did, Juan saw that she had an injured hand; evidently she had somehow mangled it. *That'll hinder her at work*, he thought, almost tenderly, as though she were related to him.

He went to the till, tallied up his takings, and said to the owner, "See you tomorrow." Quickly, he left.

Luisa sat on a while longer, deep in thought.

Just then a very young girl stepped lightly from the kitchen. She was remarkably beautiful: she had the sort of beauty that can banish thoughts of pain. One man asked another who she was. "Juan's daughter, Susanna."

Susanna changed the glasses on Luisa's table. "My father's expecting you at San Anton quay," she said.

Luisa ran to the place Susanna had indicated.

Juan regarded her steadily. "Your Cristobal got lucky," he said. "Although he met with a suspect in our café, he managed to escape. He's sailed on the first ship. Being smart, as he is, he'll soon find the right connections in Florida."

"When will he return?"

"Hopefully not so soon. If times remain as they are, he's sure to be under suspicion. And what'll his friend, the one they lifted, say about him?"

Luisa's eyes had stayed as dry as tinder throughout her separation from Cristobal. "When do you think something will change around here?" she asked Juan.

"When our Bébé Doc has gone. Perhaps not even then. For us, now, the greatest danger is Vodou, which masquerades as the people's religion. The Vodouists hate the Catholics, and the Catholics hate the Vodouists."

"I understand little of it now that my boyfriend's no longer here. He used to explain everything to me."

"Then you're not doing very well, my girl. You must remain the person he held dear; otherwise he'll stop longing for you."

"Explain a little to me, Juan."

"What is there to explain? Papa Doc thought to do the pagans some good: he declared the old superstitions, the Vodou beliefs, to be the state religion. When we were slaves, Vodou meant something else to us entirely. The old Vodou gods summoned us into the forest by night. We sang, we danced; we cursed our masters who granted us not a moment's happiness. That's all changed now. Bébé Doc, his son, wants everyone to sing the pagan songs again, like we did as slaves—but whether slaves or workers, it won't make our lives any easier."

"And he himself, Bébé Doc, what does he believe?"

"Whatever makes him most money. Now Christians have to watch their backs when they help the poor. But our poor are completely ignorant; they pray to the pagan gods together with their masters, the Duvaliers. And the Duvaliers are afraid a new Cuba will arise here."

"Is Cristobal far away now?" Luisa asked.

"I think he's safe. He's one of the lucky ones."

"She's beautiful, your daughter. May she be happier in love than I."

"You should both be happy. We cannot live without happiness."

From then on Luisa often went alone to the café opposite

the African museum. Susanna would tell her where her father Juan was expecting her. "In all that you do," Juan told Luisa, "you have to imagine that Cristobal is telling you to do it."

*T*hrough her window, Luisa could have studied any customer who stopped in front of Mr. Lopez's store. She could have regularly taken a break to scrutinize the people who went up to see her boss. *What drives this lovely girl to grind away like this in my office?* Lopez wondered at times.

Luisa was startled when from the room next door came a familiar voice. Hugs and exclamations followed.

"Send it all to me at Plaza Melchor Ocampo, number nine."

"So, Cristobal, that's your new place?"

"Yes, we've finally moved here. Mania realizes I need to live here. Her father grants her every wish. Without his help we could never have set up the library, where you can borrow virtually anything you want—French, English, Spanish, even Russian. The Party would never have accomplished that with its own resources. The library's open three times a week. On Sundays we'll hold lectures there, too."

They left the building. Luisa grabbed a scarf at random and tied it round her head. She walked closely after them to the jetty, then behind them over the pontoon. She pulled the scarf down, completely masking her face. She listened carefully to both men.

"Look," said Lopez. "Over there, the ship's about to disappear over the horizon. You've made this journey twice already. Wouldn't you like to sail today?"

"Yes and no," replied Cristobal. "Yes and no." And he added after a short pause, "I belong here, do you understand? Perhaps beaten to death, perhaps bleeding to death in a ditch, but here. Do you understand me?"

Lopez said nothing.

"I can accomplish more here with our library than we ever could have previously. We needn't worry whether people guess as to Mania's father's involvement. Mania knows how to talk him into anything—that's a tremendous boon for our stricken country."

Until now Luisa's heart had been still. Suddenly it awoke to a reality that was hard to bear.

"Do you really believe Cristobal came to use his father-in-law's money for our country?" Luisa asked the waiter, Juan, whom she met with afterwards.

"Or for your sake?" replied Juan. "That too is possible. Or perhaps for both reasons. You mustn't on any account bother him with such questions, do you understand?"

Later, Mr Lopez told Luisa to drive to Cristobal's apartment in Plaza Melchor Ocampo to check over the order. But Luisa replied that she had a job to do in town just then, and besides, she would check the delivery thoroughly at the packing stage.

She didn't think that Cristobal had seen her, or that he knew she worked for Lopez. Cristobal, for his part, did not know whether Luisa had any idea of his return, or had perhaps even heard from the talk that he had come home married to a rich and beautiful woman.

It was always possible that both had some inkling, and longed for each other.

One Sunday morning Cristobal went up the stairs to the library with his wife, right before Luisa's eyes. Luisa noted how lovely Mania's legs were, how well dressed she was.

It was around then that the *Tontons Macoutes*, the secret police, began to rampage through the city: into shops, huts, and houses, into studios, salons, and factories; they stormed the libraries, trampled books, seized people here and there and tossed them down stairs and into vans. They swept through the city as far as the main jail, yelling and cheering for the Duvaliers.

Cristobal and Mania were not harassed. Two police guards ordered them to get into their own car. Beside the chauffeur sat a police officer in dark glasses. They were driven to Florida quay. There they were escorted onto a ship.

Luisa was immediately taken for interrogation. She waited impassively, without fear. She ought to have been worried, but felt only a mild sense of surprise. She was asked who had referred her to this library, who the librarian was, and where she had made her acquaintance. Luisa shrugged her shoulders. Finally, as again she shrugged to the same questions, she received a lash of the whip that tore her dress; then a further lash, by whom Luisa could not have said, since the man whipping her stood out of sight behind her. She was dragged in bloodied rags to a stinking cell that echoed with cries and moans. But, waking from her dazed state, she felt a certain pride, because she had kept quiet. *When Juan hears, he'll be pleased with me.* Luisa did not think *Cristobal*; rather, *Juan*. She thought her wounds stung less fiercely, and the moaning in the cell abated a little.

In order to torment individual prisoners indiscriminately

and thus keep them all in a perpetual state of fear, now this prisoner, now that prisoner was ordered to empty the filthy cell pit, even to clean it. Above them, on a platform where the stench was less pervasive, stood several guards, jeering and laughing. It amused them to see a pretty face, a naked arm besmirched.

One day another prisoner was lowered on a rope, due to her defiance or for some other reason. To the guards' surprise, she swiftly untied the knot at her belt. Instantly she was up to her hips in filth. She grabbed a long-handled shovel and paddled over to Luisa. Luisa recognized her; she had done some work in Lopez's office, months or weeks before. Luisa sensed that this new prisoner—her name was Amalia—wanted to tell her something important. Once they were standing together, Amalia, almost fainting from the stench, leaned over to Luisa. "You know, soon it'll be curtains for that band of Duvaliers. They say Bébé Doc lies at death's door; smallpox hasn't spared him."

"And what'll happen then?"

"Presumably something better; something else, at any rate."

The prisoners were soon to see the guards, sensing their imminent demise, let off steam one more time in a frenzy of fear.

*M*eanwhile Cristobal had moved to France. Around this time he was sitting with his wife, Mania, at a café on the Boulevard Saint-Germain in Paris. He was reading over a letter from home.

"What's new?" his wife asked.

"Nothing." After a pause Cristobal said, "Mania, I think we've been here long enough."

"Why?" his young wife asked, dismayed. "Here there's peace and quiet. What do you call home? Haiti? It's just one big cauldron of fear and intimidation. What do you want there? Have you forgotten what awaits you? Just imagine borrowing a book from a banned library—if you're caught, you're locked up. You can no longer conceive what kind of a country it is. For instance, you go into a bookshop—that one opposite—and already they're on your trail. They'll seize us, take us away."

Cristobal listened in amusement. "Nonsense," he replied. "Your father will help us as long as there are these Duvaliers. With that kind of safeguard, why not do the right thing for your country, back home?"

"Do the right thing for your country, back home?" repeated Mania, stupefied.

Two Hispano-African students with their briefcases passed, through the shimmering, golden autumn air. "Look at that beauty!" said one to the other. Mania understood the words, even though they had been uttered in Spanish. Her eyes flashed.

"You know what?" said Cristobal. "Perhaps I'll go on ahead. When your father and I think it bearable for you, you can follow on."

Mania was silent for a moment. Then she blurted, "Neither of you can make me. Surely you must have another, particular reason to return to that dreadful island. Perhaps you've a girlfriend there from before. Tell me honestly."

"No," Cristobal replied. "Then I wouldn't have traveled so

far away for so long."

*I*n Haiti, the prisoners broke free after first the prison gate was forced open, then one cell after another. Those who were not so weak and wounded that their families had to carry them home plunged into the river of people, into its singing and rejoicing. They were convinced a new life awaited them, one entirely different to the old, insufferable one.

At the prison there were several repulsive guards who had tucked themselves away in various nooks and crannies. As the river of people left the prison behind, intent upon storming the main prison by the sea, sweeping up all those who had only moments ago been incarcerated and terrified of interrogation and torture, these killers, the guards at the besieged prison, realized that they would probably have to believe in this new life if they were recognized here or outside. They knew there were secret cells for special prisoners. As the triumphant procession left the street behind, these guards did what the people joyously surging forward had prevented before: they unlocked the hidden cells and turned on the forgotten prisoners. They trampled them, slashed them, mutilated them. Then they made off, through courtyards and over walls.

Triumphantly, amid singing and rejoicing, the procession advanced along the main street. Cristobal and Juan—whom Cristobal had recognized by his gold-buttoned jacket—joined the procession, because in the prison Juan had failed to find the woman he had been frantically searching for, either among the surviving prisoners or the murdered.

"You were often in the café opposite the African museum," said Juan. Then, after a pause, he added, "Did you come back from Cuba for the liberation?" In his voice there was a trace of scorn that Cristobal did not quite catch. "To liberate us, or to join the liberation?" Juan continued. "I served you there again, that last time. They dragged your friend away. I don't know what happened to your bride."

"Which bride?"

"Luisa. I'd hoped we'd find her. She must be hiding in some hole in the basement, since she wasn't in any of the cells. Maybe she's been taken somewhere else. Perhaps even killed."

A chill went down Cristobal's spine. He fell silent.

The people's procession reached the shore, singing, chanting furiously: "The new man will be another altogether!" — "Just as long as he's not Grandson Doc!" Some boats were sailing to San Jago peninsula. That was where the main prison was. From the sea it presented a sheer, impenetrable, smooth-sided rock topped with crags; its cells were windowless except for the holes through which the inner courtyard cobbles could be seen. This prison had been hated above all from time immemorial, even before the Papa Doc era. The horror was heightened by the fact that every prisoner there knew, sensed through and through, how close liberated Cuba was—a boat journey away beyond windowless walls.

In their hope (and at the same time fear) of finding Luisa here, Juan and Cristobal plunged toward the departure point, breaking through the front rows so as not to miss the first steamboat. But just short of the jetty, both men stopped in their tracks. They pushed no farther forward. Suddenly they looked each other in the eye.

Cristobal grabbed Juan by the arm; he inclined his head as he listened to something indefinable in the city. Anguished cries, now drowned by the talking around them, now clear and pronounced, reached them from the place they had only just left.

"You hear it?" Cristobal asked.

"Now I hear it, yes," Juan replied, after a short silence.

Juan was not surprised when, rather than take the next boat, Cristobal turned around. They shoved their way back with all their might. "Where to? Why back?" the parading people demanded angrily, cursing indignantly before closing rank once more. Juan and Cristobal pushed through time and again until they were back before the old prison gate.

They showed the guards—these were now guards of the people—some papers. Finally, the two of them rushed back into the prison they had besieged with the multitude an hour before. Again Cristobal grabbed Juan by the arm. Again they looked each other in the eye. At the same time both heard, not loud, but clearly perceptible: "Come back! Don't leave me!"

They descended to the basement. After a moment's hesitation Juan said, "I can hear it again."

"So can I," said Cristobal.

They followed a moaning that they heard, or thought they heard: "Don't go! Don't go!" Then it was quiet again, as though they had only been dreaming; but it drew them through the cold corridor they had only recently run along, searching in vain. On the floor lay bloodied rags. Presumably the last prisoners had been beaten or trampled here.

All at once the basement was silent and still. Cristobal and Juan looked at each other, at a loss. Turn back? Was it all a bad dream? Then at the same time both heard, somewhere nearby: "I'm here. Stay."

Juan, who always grasped everything a moment before Cristobal, said decisively, "We're staying, Luisa. We're getting you out. Don't be afraid."

Battered bodies strewed the corridor. Blood was flowing from a girl's stomach and face. She was too weak to move; she could have been taken for dead. Cristobal tried to brush away the hair matted to her face. He stared at what was revealed. He shuddered in fear and horror. Gingerly Juan took her hand. It seemed to him that one finger had once been crushed. "It's Luisa," he said emphatically. "I recognize her by her hand."

"Are you quite sure?" Cristobal asked.

She flinched in pain at the slightest touch.

"She often had coffee at our café," Juan said. "Among a thousand hands, I would recognize hers." Her previously gentle face was disfigured, destroyed.

They carried Luisa out of the prison. "We're taking her to mine," Juan insisted.

Somehow they tried to bathe the blood-encrusted woman. Luisa moaned in pain with every movement.

Juan knew a doctor who was too old to take part in the procession, and sent for him. He cleaned the worst of her wounds. Carefully he brought her back to the point where she could talk again.

Now she lay quiet and still in Juan's hut.

"Do you really think it's her?" Cristobal shivered as he asked

Juan.

"I know it is," he replied. "I recognize her by her hand. She often paid for her coffee at ours. I lit her cigarettes."

Luisa groaned even if Cristobal barely touched her. Her face would contort into a grimace.

Susanna came back from school. She already knew what had happened in the city, and whom her parents were sheltering. The first time she saw Luisa she was seized with horror. Soon she became her best nurse.

Life in Haiti calmed down. Of course, no one could say for certain how it would turn out in the end. Juan regularly argued with Cristobal and many other friends, and all who joined them still spoke with some caution about events. Would Vodou, which had formerly drawn black people into the forest during the slavery era, remain the state religion? For the moment the president not only tolerated Vodou, but encouraged it. Could they exist side by side, the old slavery beliefs and Catholic Christianity?

Apart from those who loitered around the harbor or queued to look for work, many went about their business again. Cristobal was appointed head teacher in the inner city; Juan returned to being a waiter in the café across from the African Museum; the library, where previously various books had been secretly hidden, now held as its main stock the very books that had been banned.

Luisa remained a permanent testimony to the acts of persecution she had suffered. Her face grew calm and happy when Cristobal caressed her mutilated hand. She was still so weak that his caress caused her more pain than pleasure. She expected him at a set time of day; you saw that in her face, even though the abuse had left it a disfigured mask. Perhaps only Susanna understood what went on inside her.

So that Luisa could sleep comfortably, they used bamboo to section off a narrow area of Susanna's father's small, one-roomed hut.

Sometimes the teacher Sophia came by. Every time she saw her friend, she had to overcome her horror. She drew Cristobal aside. "How do you see things continuing for you two? You're not thinking of moving into your own house, marrying her, are you? You'll have to constantly steel yourself to stand the sight of her. Think about it!"

Another time Juan talked to his friend. "There was a woman from the USA who often used to sit in my café," he told Cristobal. "Her face was disfigured in a car crash. So she went home to a famous doctor. He fixed her face, so to speak. When she returned she was more beautiful than before the accident. Surely it can't be hard to find such a doctor."

"I'd never do such a thing to Luisa!" Cristobal said. "Quite the opposite—I'm proud of these scars; whoever sees them will know how they came about."

Juan said nothing.

Sometimes Luisa was able to get up and give Juan's wife a hand. This made her happy, but she had to hide how quickly she tired. She needed all her energy just to receive Cristobal sitting up rather than lying flat on her bed.

Juan and his wife kept an eye on everything. They worried

about the future Luisa and Cristobal would soon face; which, essentially, they already faced. Their daughter Susanna had heard all their conversations, or at least guessed that they concerned her too; her parents had noticed how often Cristobal cast the girl an admiring glance or tried to brush her arm.

Once, when Susanna brought the meal for Cristobal and Luisa, Luisa said in a clear and firm voice, "I want to say something to you both. Please stay by my bed.

"We are all three fond of each other. Cristobal, you know how distraught I was that time, when you sailed to Cuba and we had to part. Perhaps I despaired even more when you returned but soon after went away again with a woman I didn't know. Juan grasped everything back when they arrested Paolo, and you, Cristobal, left again—for years, we thought.

"Now you've come back again and found me as, let's face it, the wrecked, ruined creature I now am and shall remain."

Susanna made to soothe Luisa, who had already talked too much. In her excitement Luisa's scarred face looked particularly ghastly, almost grotesque.

"My children, we cannot live without happiness. You, Cristobal, need Susanna. It would give me great joy if I could stay near you both so that Susanna could help me, as she's done up until now. All told, that would honestly be the greatest of joys for me."

Susanna and Cristobal made no reply. Luisa had not expected a swift response. She pretended to sleep.

During the night, in their half of the hut, Susanna's parents had listened to this conversation and other similar ones. The very possibility of such a marriage, to which Susanna seemed

not unduly opposed, displeased them. Although Cristobal at first firmly refused, but then considered it at length and did not dismiss the idea entirely, they considered a relationship between him and their daughter out of the question. To their minds it was a disgrace to abandon the woman; the very idea undermined the whole point of Luisa's rescue.

But Luisa, in a concerted effort which almost wore her out, reiterated to Susanna's parents what she had already made clear to the other two: Susanna and Cristobal belonged together; this relationship made her, Luisa, happy.

The neighbors muttered as the new way of life began. But soon it was clear to everyone that Cristobal and Susanna had become husband and wife, and Luisa remained in their care.

One day Cristobal bumped into Mania's father. The latter told Cristobal that his daughter had met someone in Paris and did not intend to return to Haiti.

Coming home from his work in the café, Juan would often sit with Luisa, and to cheer her up, would tell her about all his weird and wonderful customers. Gently he probed Luisa and tried to ascertain how she was coming to terms with her new life.

On one occasion, Luisa's tone changed. She said, with that smile which, although it could no longer make her face beautiful, did brighten it, "Didn't you always say to me that we cannot live without happiness? There's a joy that radiates from inside a person, such that it too can thrill you and make you happy."

Juan lowered his pained expression. He made no response to Luisa's thoughts.

During the short rainy season followed by a hot, dry spell and then the long rainy season, Luisa was urged by everyone to stay indoors. Nevertheless, when she was alone—with Cristobal at school and Susanna at the market—she tried to take some air. Soon after, she began to cough. The doctor could not help her. The coughing hurt, almost like torture. It was a relief to her to die a swift death.

She was given a fine funeral procession in which all those who had shared her thoughts took part. As they walked along, these thoughts began to take root.

Great, Unknown Men: A Black Man against Napoleon (1948)

On one of the first Columbus ships sailed a Spanish monk by the name of Las Casas, who later became Bishop of Chiapas, a southern province of Mexico. His first impression of the native inhabitants of the Antilles may have resembled the one Columbus described in his letter to the Spanish royal court: such gentle, childlike people, so biddable and clever, such as one does not encounter in Europe; this newly discovered world so rich and enchanting, like the Garden of Eden. It seems Columbus really did deem this a land worthy of holy salvation, unsullied and unstained by the sins and vices of the West; to win so many meek, innocent children for baptism, he thought at the time, made the tribulations of his discovery voyage worthwhile.

But Las Casas was soon to taste bitter disappointment. The Spanish officers and soldiers were more concerned about gold than about saving souls. Before their arrival, the indigenous peoples had gone down the mine only after prayer to dig gold for their temple treasures; now, they were set upon by dogs, chained together and coerced into forced labor until they gave up the ghost. In the first stages of the *conquista* there were Spanish nobles who made it their goal to dispatch twelve natives before breakfast—for, they reasoned, twelve was the number of the apostles.

This was a different concept of Christianity to the one that Las Casas had formed in his heart, and in the hearts of the people he wished to educate. Legend lives on today of his wisdom and goodness. Despite this, he too was testament to the word of St Paul, which is, as far as we know and can say, fragmented. Las Casas loved the indigenous people so much that his power of imagination was bound to their fate; thus is his name to be found clearly signed alongside other, less clear names, at the bottom of a document approving the introduction of black people from Africa (because, it was said, this race was better adapted to the rigors of the climate than the indigenous peoples).

The importation of blacks to the Caribbean began at the start of the sixteenth century. It rose to 30,000 annually in the eighteenth century, a century which owes to its philosophers the title of "The Age of Philanthropy." The ships that transported the slaves from assembly camps on the African coast to their destinations were worse than floating concentration camps. On every voyage, a high percentage of dead were included in the trade balance. The blacks in Africa were either hunted down by whites, or traded by tribal chiefs from their stock of captives from other tribes or from their own surplus stock. Certain shrewd or talented tribes were favored more than others.

In the colonies, a distinction was made between the recently imported African blacks and the so-called creoles who had been born there. The endorsement bearing Las Casas's signature was right in one regard: the blacks were unbelievably strong and incredibly fertile. From an economic standpoint, plantation owners preferred their slaves to be unmarried because church marriage forbade the separation of couples, individual slaves being supplied on demand to the various estates.

For the mass deployment of slave labor was preceded by one other mass act: mass baptism. However, this did not subdue the blacks' remembrance of their ancient gods: the Vodou cult drew blacks again and again, particularly in times of turmoil, into the forest, to forbidden altars honoring their secret priests.

From the confusion that ensued after the *conquista*, which Spain quelled from its position of power, the island of Hispaniola was left with two faces: a Spanish and a French side. "War, trade, and piracy, they are a triune, never to be separate." (*Faust*, Act II). The Spanish territory remained thinly populated pastureland; its capital, Santo Domingo, which Columbus's brother originally founded, had never recovered from being burned down by a great buccaneer.

On the French half of Hispaniola, by the eighteenth century Saint-Domingue had become one of the jewels in the French royal crown. Under the security of the homeland, numerous towns and powerful, fortified estates had grown from the scattered settlements established by roving adventurers. In Le Cap, Port-au-Prince and other towns, there were shops, fashions and festivals comparable with those of Paris. The aristocrats had themselves a jolly holiday when they came from France to settle accounts with the administrators. The revenue required for their ardent and refined lifestyle was budgeted for by these administrators from slave labor on the estates. Once upon a time the gold mining of the indigenous peoples had disappointed the Spanish; before long, the figures from the plantations exceeded all expectations. France secured its colonial status through what it made in terms of profit from sugar (sugar cane was introduced from Brazil), coffee, cocoa, tobacco, indigo, and other luxury goods that flourished in Saint-Domingue.

At first the instruction was to give black slaves enough land to cultivate to feed themselves. This was to include enough time to work their land. Thus, the degree of freedom they craved was initially no more than the requisite freedom to work, which was granted to them under the "Code Noir", the edict of the king. This left the blacks with the vague image of a distant, glorious, probably benevolent ruler, cruelly duped by his colonial officials who were less concerned about the wellbeing of his subjects.

The aristocratic estate owners, called *grands blancs*, had brought with them to the colony a trail of *petits blancs*, whose existence depended upon the economic necessities of administrators, shops and businesses; or at least, they pinned their hopes upon such necessities if they could find no other livelihood back home. As an intermediate class they enjoyed a certain amount of contact with one further class which, due to skin color and economic status, lay between white landowners and black slaves: the mulattos, who were positioned between above and below, between white and black, with origins in both. Their children did not fall under the slave statute of the black parent; they could, with time, work their way up to better positions. A proportion managed thus to acquire land and status in the business world. Some even managed to achieve economic superiority over *petits blancs*. The mulattos longed to be free of the burdensome restrictions the law imposed on their caste, excluding them from the privileges of the whites.

Regarding the colonial race issue, which at times became particularly clear in Saint-Domingue, one sees that skin color can express a social stratum—as in certain chemistry experiments when, say, the litmus paper indicates acidity level through the degree of coloration.

On a rich and renowned farm belonging to a French aristocratic family from Bréda, a boy who was at first called Pierre Simon grew up in the slave quarters. He was an earnest boy, lean and tough. The Bréda farm-estate administrator was under instruction not to be hard on the slaves. When it emerged that young Simon had a craving for education, he was allowed to learn to read and write with the Jesuits. Later he was allowed to borrow books from the administrator's library. His education, though not substantial, considerably surpassed that of people of his status. From his religious teachers he also obtained a different concept of Christianity to that which mass baptism had imparted to his fellow sufferers. His whole life long, he never forgot that one of the three holy kings—who had been drawn by the same star from three points of the compass to lay their gifts before the Christ child—had been black like himself.

Pierre Simon knew how to handle animals, especially horses, both healthy and sick. He became a coachman. He started a family. He lived a quiet and carefree life with his wife and their handful of children. "He had made it beyond mid-life," as they say. Things might have carried on in this vein; he was close to reaching the conclusion that things could be better for all blacks if all owners treated their slaves humanely and considerately, as his owner did him. The conclusion stood to reason, tantalizingly so, but he had yet to reach it.

On his coach box he listened to the same conversations as the other domestic slaves when they lined up along the tables to serve at banquets, a black behind every chair. In the evenings around the fire and in the slave quarters he heard how blacks reimagined the incidents related at the table. Among other cases, he might have heard that nobleman Le Jeune had tortured slaves to death, including two women; they died from burns and lacerations, in chains with iron collars. When Le Jeune was charged, the colonists ensured his acquittal.

Or the case of Macandal, a fugitive shepherd who gathered around him bands of fugitive slaves. He distributed arsenic to them in order to carry out a poisoning campaign in the city of Le Cap. He was captured and died at the stake. The blacks told the story of his escape and of his transformation into a mosquito.

The French king with his "Code Noir" restricted the whites' right to punish to fifty whip lashes. At least that was moderate enough, when one considered the cruelty of white women who had their female slaves virtually flogged to death for burning cakes.

Reports from the latest ship's crews provided the best material for the blacks' imagination and speculation. Serfdom in France? It appeared some whites had it no better there than blacks here; otherwise, why would they want freedom? It was reported that the king had had to convene the National

Assembly.

The *Club Massaic* demanded the French colony's independence and for landowners to be represented in the assembly. They had no wish to fall under the jurisdiction of the new laws, which to them seemed unacceptable for their own businesses—for the slaves had unexpected friends in Paris: Lafayette, Robespierre, to name but a few, who had founded the Society of the Friends of the Blacks.

There also existed in Paris—where apparently there existed everything under the sun—a Mulatto Club. It fought for mulattos' equality. A rich young mulatto, Ogé, came clandestinely to Saint-Domingue, and armed his people, mulattos and black slaves. He was captured and executed.

All this Pierre Simon heard, sometimes behind him on his box, sometimes recounted around him in the evenings. And everything was embellished and enhanced by the unstoppable desire to dance, by songs that never ceased (neither round the fire at night, nor during the day at work), by the distant drumming of Vodou priests who led the pagan cult that the whites had never fully eradicated—not least because their Christian teachings with its core message of inner freedom all too often seemed to be of no benefit to black slaves.

Before long the rich whites of Saint-Domingue were no longer a self-contained body. The party that was pushing for the colony's independence stood in opposition to the pro French government party. Perhaps it was the pro-government support that encouraged the other party's black slaves to abandon the estates and flee into the jungle. The fires were started more swiftly, more systematically than had been expected. Manor houses and plantations went up in flames.

Pierre Simon led his family to safety, along with that of his owner. Suddenly, the treasure trove of experiences that each person garners over a life and usually takes with them to the grave, unappreciated and unacknowledged, was urgently called to the fore. Simon felt he was no longer right to hide his own treasure, even though at heart he liked the quiet, reflective life. He sensed his hour had come. He went the way the others had gone. He made for the jungle. He arrived at the blacks' main camp.

He had no desire to fight the black leaders, who had assembled this camp, for rank and title. To fit with form, first he let them appoint him head doctor. At any rate, there were neither hospitals nor medical supplies. The gathered slaves were still more or less a band, in rags if not completely naked, apart from a few uniformed officers with sabers. Simon neither sought nor found time to apply the little medical knowledge he possessed. He began at once to tirelessly drill what was initially a small troop of blacks until he had made soldiers out of them.

Agents sent from Paris to mediate reconciliation—for too forcible a change could have triggered the downfall of this most valuable of colonies—tried to initiate talks between the estate owners and the slave leaders. But every agreement failed in the face of the owners' intransigence. They refused, as before, to acknowledge the new mulatto law which the National Assembly had now endorsed. They were not even prepared to allow any concessions to the runaway slaves. "We haven't imported half a million blacks only to make them citizens of France," was their retort. They thought they could maintain this attitude undisturbed on their remote island until the storm in Paris had died down. There, the aristocrats were being imprisoned. There, the king was arrested on the run.

News of the king's beheading shocked Pierre Simon almost as deeply as it did the rulers in Saint-Domingue, who refused to swap the lily banner for the Tricolore. A king! To Simon he was the descendent of the three holy kings, one of whom had been black like himself. He led his guerrillas on secret night marches into the Spanish half of Hispaniola. A Christian king still ruled there, so he believed; his officials' assurances still held legal validity. Simon had no faith in a fledgling French Republic which, in the name of freedom, had executed a king and yet did not possess sufficient power to implement freedom in Saint-Domingue.

The National Convention provided the newly appointed people's commissioners with a regiment of revolutionary soldiers. Their position was virtually hopeless at first. They were attacked from all sides. The English had occupied several of the ports. The landowners encouraged, indeed, requested them to do so. The *grands blancs* preferred to do business under English rule than under the freedom of French Jacobins. The *petits blancs* were embittered against the new mulatto law; it had robbed them of their outright privilege—the privilege of being white. The mulattos were satisfied with the new law, but they had demanded it in order to enjoy unrestricted economic access, like the whites. They were, from top to bottom, anti Jacobin freedom.

The commissioners were at their wits' end. They, along with their soldiers, were quickly forced into a corner. The English helped with bribery, to spare their people. When the people's commissioners received monetary offers, they answered the English by challenging them to a duel. The commissioners' situation was politically and militarily hopeless. If they were to plant the Tricolore in Saint-Domingue, there was only one source of help, and it too looked to be lost: the blacks who had liberated themselves.

By this time Pierre Simon had trained his guerrillas. They made astonishing advances. They obeyed his word. Any pillaging, any violation was forbidden. Simon had already realized that his hope in the Spanish had been misplaced. The assurances resulting from his defection applied only to him and his men, rather than to all blacks. Where the English had joined forces with the Spanish, the slave trade remained in place, unrestricted. Simon saw his mistake. With his soldiers he contrived his second secret volte-face. He offered his services to the French commissioners. Whether Saint-Domingue remained with the French Republic now depended on the blacks. It all hinged on whether Pierre Simon comprehended that the blacks would be free if they fought for the Republic. A few days after Simon's defection, the edict of the people's commissioners, namely, the abolition of slavery, was declared as law. After doubt, confusion and detour, the Revolution had been realized through the skill of this one man.

In subsequent battles, in conversations and song, in letters and decrees, Pierre Simon was given the name Toussaint Louverture, a name that has often, but never fully, been explained. Toussaint-Simon, after defecting to the side of the commissioners, repels the English to the outermost ports with his black troops, who are poorly equipped and clothed only in rags. He defeats the Spanish with whom the English have united. By means of the new colonial committee and the *sûreté publique* he pushes through, in the face of hatred and opposition, the assurances he made to imprisoned aristocrats to spare their lives and those of their families. The commissioners are far too indebted to him to disregard his assurances. We already see at this early stage of his career that Toussaint is trying to bring conflicting elements to a common denominator, in order to organize the state system that he envisions for this island. A report at the time stated: "For his opponents, the compromises, conflicts and negotiations are intended to postpone and reverse the abolition of slavery. For Toussaint, they only serve to validate its abolition."

In the south of the island Toussaint found an adversary, who for a time was his rival by virtue of his cunning and resolve, and also thanks to the counter-warning contained in his answers to the same questions: the mulatto Rigaud. As champion of his intermediate class, Rigaud wished to grant privilege neither to blacks nor whites. He even found approbation among a small group of free blacks who owed their long years of freedom not to slavery's abolition, but to individual acts by individual slave owners. For instance, Jesuits often released slaves who had served their order. What Rigaud demanded was neither the eradication of the whites nor the reintroduction of slavery; rather, a sort of class system wherein the three skin colors held their legitimacy, but in which the mulattos would govern. He employed no end of tricks to turn the population against Toussaint. He had a shipment of chains brought ashore as evidence that Toussaint was planning a new wave of enslavement. When people's commissioner Laveaux visited the city of Le Cap, under Rigaud's orders the mulatto governor set upon him and had him imprisoned. Laveaux was freed through Toussaint's intervention.

The Revolution had, from its inception to the Directorate, at every stage of its manifestation, posted commissioners to Saint-Domingue. What kind of men these were could be seen from their conduct toward Toussaint, who took every situation to a head and forced his partners to take a stance. Commissioner Laveaux sailed back in friendship to France as candidate for the senate. Ever since Toussaint had become the only possible fulcrum of the Revolution, so shrewdly, so unconditionally had he championed its founding principles of freedom and equality that, slowly but surely, its unimpeded implementation brought its dangers for the Motherland. The principles now being enshrined in Saint-Domingue were crumbling in France. At the time, Saint-Domingue was the leading center of trade in the West. It boasted the highest coffee and sugar production. Thanks to Toussaint it had not been lost—neither to the colonial aristocracy, nor to England nor to Spain. It could yet be lost in a different way through independence under reckless, inexperienced leadership.

Not every agent would be sent home as easily as Laveaux. A certain Sonthonax was less attracted by the honor of being the candidate from Saint-Domingue. He had a foothold in every Saint-Domingue class. He had endorsed equality for the mulattos. He was the first to distribute weapons to black workers. He was ambitious, passionate about the task he had been sent out to do. It was he who suggested Toussaint establish a purely black state on the island through the eradication of the whites. "To put Toussaint to the test," as he later claimed.

"But what, then, should happen with you, citizen?" Toussaint ought to have responded.

Commissioner Sonthonax probably considered himself the only possible inspiration, and the former black slaves merely his instrument. Eventually, by force and by cunning, Toussaint sent this man packing, too, on a ship to France. There Sonthonax declared of him: "He's already made fools of two kings, and now a republic."

Sonthonax's successor attempted, by order of the Directorate, to get rid of the bold and bothersome Toussaint and his black army. He diverted Toussaint's attention to places where the liberation of blacks was still pending: Jamaica, other islands of the Antilles, South American states. To Toussaint it seemed more beneficial to first and foremost ensure that on his island, slavery would never return. To this end he engaged in battles, trickery, alliances, a degree of back and forth, a secret accord with England (which was still at war with France), and also the protection of the cities that the English themselves had called for. He knew full well that a tiny black state could only maintain its freedom with care and compliance. He did not care about people casting aspersions. He was used to it. In his private offices he granted preference to whites over mulattos. He knew that without whites, he could not operate in a white world; once won over, they were a safer bet than mulattos. The Directorate's envoy, Hedouville, tried—for every diversion had been to no avail—to play mulattos against blacks. Roume, who was commissioner then, called this method "Machiavellian and unrepublican." The island creaked once more under internal conflict. The mulattos were released. Rigaud fled to Paris. There, Bonaparte, who had been appointed first consul, heard his complaints. "I see only one error in you: you were defeated," Bonaparte responded.

*T*he Revolution had ground to a standstill. Bonaparte held true to that which served him—his need for power and glory. What in France signified a backward step, when set against the achievements of the Revolution, its meager scraps, had a renewed and startling effect in the reactionary, unyielding states that Napoleon and his army later occupied. Toussaint was just then at the peak of his own powers. In 1800 he had the island in his hands. The churches held services of thanksgiving. The entire population, black, white and mixed race, lauded he who had brought about peace. The towns and plantations that had suffered in the war prospered again. Toussaint even encouraged those landowners not facing serious incrimination to return— but no longer as slave owners, for he had placed freedom to work under legal protection. He also forced blacks by law to take up work again for payment, with restricted freedom of movement; for years, in wartime, they had been used to an itinerant life. He allowed into office whites, mulattos and blacks according to their expertise. They wrote to Paris about his leadership: "The races melt like wax in his hands." He no longer wore a kerchief wrapped around his head, as he once had as a slave; he had the bearing of a people's servant. And his black fellow workers followed suit. At first, they were in wonderment abroad at the little black miracle; then they were perplexed. The economy rose to nearly its previous level. The whole island celebrated Toussaint's new constitution. Previously he might have needed the seal of approval from Paris for this celebration. Now, he only let it be known after its implementation.

Napoleon had long refused to ever tolerate epaulettes on the shoulders of blacks. From the outset it was clear to him that he had to erase this runaway black. He simply visualized the task in relation to his conquest of the rest of the world; even though later, on St. Helena, he would happen to say that he might have done better not to meddle with Toussaint, he was nevertheless aware of the innumerable external necessities for his attack. But not of the deeper why: that he faced a seemingly insignificant black opponent on a remote island who wished, as stubbornly as he did and with similar cunning, to apply opposing principles. Napoleon's contemporaries adjudged that, above all, his concern was to prevent France from losing the island. There were a few other not fully clarified, less-important reasons, too: his wife's Martinique ancestry and landholdings in the Antilles, which meant she was not uninvolved in the plantation economy; also, his wish to compensate the Vendée aristocrats—who owned large plantations in Saint-Domingue—for their expropriation, but that could not happen in a volatile colony where their support for the counter-revolution was all too public.

It seems logical—aside from all the pretexts upon which Toussaint's elimination was founded—that these two men would clash, given that both thought and acted in opposing directions from opposing sets of principles. The military might lay with Napoleon. So great was this might, so vast its sphere of influence, that his opponent's name barely raised an eyebrow and was quickly forgotten... although there were and are historians who say that Napoleon's decline began not with his war against Russia, nor with the failure of his Spanish campaign, but with his assault of Haiti.

Napoleon himself imagined it would be simple, even if not all that easy; otherwise, he would not have risked as many forces as he later sent to Spain. The commander-in-chief was the husband of his favorite sister Pauline. She had been told in Paris of how lavish the receptions on the island were. She took with her a large quantity of jewelry and clothing.

This was all tarnished in the officers' tent in which she passed her time, for the city was inaccessible. Napoleon had thought the island would easily capitulate under a modern attack, an attack that would startle the blacks. He had probably imagined a kind of blitzkrieg. His armed forces, dispatched from various home-country ports to converge on Hispaniola, could not be simultaneously deployed, for they did not arrive in unison. When negotiation attempts failed, the blacks set fire to the bombarded cities themselves. When their officers gave the signal, they threw torches into their own homes.

The French had expected to end their campaign before the rainy season. The tropical rains made maneuvers and marching impossible. The blacks reverted to their old tactic: they hid in the jungle. When the people's commissioners landed, in their battle for liberation the only allies they could find were none other than the black guerrillas. The ally the blacks found, on the other hand, was none other than the scourge of the island, yellow fever: it decimated the French troops. The beautiful Pauline Bonaparte cut off her locks when her husband, the commander-in-chief, died from it.

Toussaint took up the invitation of French officers, who secured him safe passage. If one of his abilities had been weakened by the relentless, merciless battles, it was his wariness (which he retained for what remained of his life). The French paid no heed to the assurances they had given to a black man. Toussaint was immediately arrested and taken to France on a warship. He was held prisoner in a fortress on the Swiss border until his death.

*T*his did not mean the end of the defense of Haiti; only to the conception of a black state as Toussaint had planned it, as he alone could have built it—for he alone would have been capable, by dint of his intellectual and moral ability, to live, think, and learn, to bridge the gulf between his people and those who had been free for millennia.

During the first period of occupation, allegiance to Toussaint soon waned, for many blacks believed Bonaparte's allegation that Toussaint had defected from France. Bonaparte's power sufficed not only to arm the invasion militarily but also to lend it ideological impetus, by means of newspapers, pamphlets, and through rumors that his agents spread. To the blacks, France was synonymous with the French Revolution; a defection from France was a defection from its freedom laws. What had already fundamentally altered in respect of these laws under 18 Brumaire, Napoleon's coup d'état, was not immediately obvious to the blacks. Only when slavery was reintroduced on the neighboring island of Guadeloupe did they comprehend how right Toussaint had been in his warning.

They mounted a frantic resistance. Bonaparte had not bargained on the scale of it. Self-assured, hamming up the role of the individual man, whether he himself were the individual or his opponent, he had believed their resistance would soon be broken by the knowledge that he had their leader in his hands. Eventually he had to withdraw his soldiers when they became so decimated and diseased, the plantations in the former colony so forsaken and neglected, that the mission was no longer viable. Napoleon needed his available officers on other battlefields where there was scope for greater glory. Either way, the remote island was destroyed. Never again did it come anywhere close to even a fraction of its faded glory. At one time, the colonists had had the backing of one of the world's mightiest kingdoms. Toussaint's successor had no backing. He declared himself king of Haiti, which sounded not as unusual as it does today, during an era in which Emperor Napoleon made any number of officers of dubious origin his kings.

The island was soon repartitioned, in line with the two languages, into a Spanish and a French half: Santo Domingo and Haiti. Both halves were black states, nominally independent. Today, Haiti and its population, when compared with post-war Germany, experiences unimaginable poverty and misery, and depends upon foreign capital, from which only a wafer-thin upper class profits.

From time to time, from the ashes of Haitian history a spark is lit, a hint of what a son of Haiti could yet be today. *If only…* Usually the name of a friend to whom one wishes to dedicate a work is inscribed at the start. Perhaps the name of Jacques Roumain, the young and gifted Haitian poet who died a few years ago, will make more of an impression if it is placed at the end. Right here, right now, Roumain endorses with a smile this feeble, under-resourced attempt to write about the life of Toussaint, the great black leader.

Historical Context

Three Women from Haiti comprises three short stories set in three different eras of Haitian history, which collectively trace the development of revolution on the island, from pre-conquest indigenous insurrection to the overthrow of late twentieth-century military rule.

The first story, *The Hiding Place*, is set toward the end of the fifteenth century, at the start of the Spanish conquest of the Americas. Haiti's recorded history began when Christopher Columbus first arrived in December 1492. He named the island "Hispaniola" because it reminded him of Spain. Indigenous Arawak and Taino tribes were at the time organized into chiefdoms, each with their own chief. Their name for the island was "Ayiti", meaning "mountainous".

The fortress of La Navidad mentioned in *The Hiding Place* (30) was built in 1493 from wood of the shipwreck *Santa María*, near modern-day Cap-Haïtien. It was destroyed on Columbus's second visit, and all 39 Spanish settlers were killed.

Columbus's voyages of discovery came at the height of European exploration. The Spanish Crown sponsored his voyages and expected a return on their investment. A trading center was established on Hispaniola which produced luxury goods such as coffee, sugar, rum and chocolate for the European market. Indigenous people wore gold jewelry which spurred Spanish conquistadors to search for gold. They introduced to Hispaniola the *encomienda* system under which Spanish settlers were supplied with free local labor to mine gold. Intended to provide protection to local people, the system soon became an established form of slavery. Any unrest was quelled by the Spanish demanding payment of a gold tribute, and failure to pay this gold tax resulted in enforced labor in the gold mines, as mentioned in *The Hiding Place* (29).

Spanish conquistadors continued their aggressive colonizing program in Puerto Rico, Jamaica and Cuba, the pattern being conquest, settlement, exploitation of local reserves and labor, subjugation and eventual extinction of indigenous populations, including in Haiti.

Due to limited mineral resources, principally lack of gold, during the sixteenth century the Spanish gradually neglected their Caribbean colonies to pursue interests in Mexico and Latin America. This allowed rival colonizing nations, including Britain and France, to intervene in the Caribbean. After establishing a colony on the island of Tortuga, French settlers gradually encroached on the north-west of Hispaniola and formed the settlement of Cap François (later Cap Français, now Cap-Haïtien). In 1697 the French were granted sovereign control of the western half of the island, which was renamed Saint-Domingue. Under French colonial rule it became the richest colony in the world at that time, known variously as the "Pearl of the Antilles" and the "Eden of the Western World".

The establishment and development of the plantation system required mass import of slave labor from Africa. Slavery, under which people of color were legally classified as items of property, facilitated a Western, or capitalist, system of global economic expansion.

$\mathcal{T}$he failed insurrection attempt against Spanish conquistadors alluded to in *The Hiding Place* would have been one of many that several centuries later culminated in the Haitian Revolution (1791-1804). This is the focus of the second story, *The Key*, set in France at the beginning of the nineteenth century and centering on the fate of François Dominique Toussaint Louverture,[1] who rose from slave status to literate revolutionary leader. He is portrayed as Napoleon's nemesis, his rise coinciding with that of the French leader, whose decisive coup d'état on 18 Brumaire (November 9th, 1799), is referred to in *The Key* (38).

In *The Key*, the French Revolution (1787-99) is identified as the principal catalyst to liberation in Haiti. After being freed from her wall prison and joining the jubilant crowds, Claudine tells her friend Sophie: "They said that the French Revolution had liberated us; who that was, what that was, we didn't yet understand at the time. I took the Revolution to be a great big woman around whom we danced, singing." (43)

The Haitian Revolution saw the realization of French

---

1 — Upon her return to Germany from World War Two exile, Anna Seghers published a biography of Toussaint under the title *Große Unbekannte. Ein Neger gegen Napoleon* (*Great Unknowns: A Black Man Against Napoleon*) in *Ost und West* (Berlin, 1948), 2:3, pp. 51-64. Seghers subsequently used Toussaint's life story as material in a 1948 story, *A Wedding in Haiti*, the first in a trilogy of stories eventually published as *Karibische Geschichten (Caribbean Stories)* in 1962: *A Wedding in Haiti* (1948); *The Reinstatement of Slavery in Guadeloupe* (1948) ; *The Light on the Gallows: A Caribbean Tale from the Time of the French Revolution* (1960).

proletarian dreams and ideals as inscribed in the 1789 Declaration of the Rights of Man and Citizen. A nation of people primarily descended from African slaves declared themselves "human beings with significant dignity and value".[2] When the enslaved population of Saint-Domingue rose in revolt, they "interrupted the Western economy and global capitalism",[3] declaring independence from French colonial rule on 1st January 1804, creating the world's second post-colonial state (the first was North America after its independence revolution of 1783). The Haitian Revolution delivered the impossible, elusive utopian dream of emancipation.

Unlike subsequent independence movements in Latin America, which were often led by white elites, the Haitian Revolution was instigated by illiterate black slaves who freed themselves from an oppressive system. Their revolution from within has more meaning than liberation imposed from outside liberating forces.[4] The black revolutionaries renamed their liberated nation "Haiti", thereby honoring, and connecting themselves with, the vanquished indigenous population of Haiti, as portrayed in *The Hiding Place*.

Despite the Haitian Revolution being a "central world event",[5] a conspiracy of silence by France and America followed for several centuries. They wished to avoid this

---

2 — Celucien L. Joseph, "'The Haitian Turn": An Appraisal of Recent Literary and Historiographical Works on the Haitian Revolution' in *The Journal of Pan African Studies*, 5:6 (2012), pp. 37-55 (p. 38).

3 — Joseph, p. 42.

4 — Seghers had explored this idea in the second of her Caribbean stories, *The Reintroduction of Slavery on Guadeloupe*, which is critical of a nation liberated from outside without sufficient appetite to subsequently see revolutionary changes through to their end.

5 — Joseph, p. 39.

revolution becoming a "symbol of anti-colonial revolt and universal emancipation".[6] *The Key* hints at the potential, global ramifications of the Haitian Revolution when we read that news of Toussaint Louverture's death spread "everywhere that black people contemplated their fate" (48).

The ideological exclusion of the Haitian Revolution from Eurocentric, Western historiography has been readdressed in the last ten years with a "Haitian turn" being identified in Western historical scholarship,[7] and the publication of *Three Women from Haiti* in English translation represents a small but important contribution to recognizing the Haitian Revolution as a key event in world history.

The Key's French setting gives us a European perspective on events in Haiti. Mention is made of the small radical group of French writers, Society of the Friends of the Blacks (formed in 1788, outlawed by 1794), who did important work to educate Europeans as to the appalling conditions of the colonial enslaved. In *The Key*, this society is represented as an underground resistance movement. There is also allusion to resistance within the Napoleonic command in the subordination of guard Jean Violet at Fort de Joux,[8] who acts as an informer to Amédée. Mention too is made of the Jacobins, who formed clubs of radical left-wing revolutionaries in Paris and beyond during the French Revolution. Under the leadership of Robespierre, they formed a revolutionary dictatorship founded on a belief in absolute democracy. Toussaint is sometimes referred to as a

---

6 — Joseph, p. 47.

7 — See: Joseph (2012).

8 — For interesting online documentation of Toussaint's imprisonment in France, please see http://thelouvertureproject.org/index.php?title=Fort_de_Joux

"black Robespierre" as he applied the revolutionary energy of Jacobinism in Haiti.

Although the complex issue of race in Haitian society remains largely unaddressed in *The Key* (perhaps due to its foreign setting),[9] there is emphasis on the principal characters' ethnicity—black—underlining the significance of the Haitian Revolution as a black liberation movement, and the historical import of one of its principal protagonists, Toussaint Louverture. Napoleon's aversion to black people reinforces the Eurocentric setting (and contrasts with the civility and restraint with which Claudine and Amédée are portrayed). Seghers alludes to the complexity of Toussaint's position as a rebel leader, who in 1793 was allied with Royalist Spain (which still held the colony of Santo Domingo in the east, today the Spanish-speaking Dominican Republic) and led black rebels in attempting to regain Saint-Domingue from Republican French administration. In 1794 Toussaint switched loyalties to the French, principally because their administration in Haiti had abolished slavery, while Spain's had not. He was rewarded with increased powers due to his defense of French republican troops from mulatto forces, and in 1801 was named governor-general of Saint-Domingue for life. In 1802 Napoleon Bonaparte sent forces to quell Toussaint's rise to power. Two of Toussaint's lieutenants switched allegiance in the subsequent war of attrition, and Toussaint eventually surrendered.

---

9 — In *A Wedding in Haiti*, Anna Seghers offers a fictionalized representation of 18th century Haitian society which brings out the nuances of race under slavery at the time. An important third ethnic group was the mulatto, offspring of white plantation owners and African slaves. In terms of a social ladder, mulattos (some of whom held land and wealth) were positioned between black slaves on the lowest rung and white colonists on the highest.

$\mathcal{T}$he last, and longest story, *Separation*, is framed by a love story set in twentieth-century Haiti against a backdrop of military dictatorship under Bébé Doc (Jean-Claude Duvalier), who inherited power from his father, Papa Doc (François Duvalier), the son of Duval Duvalier, an immigrant from the French Caribbean colony of Martinique. During North America's neo-colonial intervention and occupation of Haiti from 1915-34, François Duvalier studied at a US-run medical school and spent a year of study in North America. The USA intervened in Haiti because of its continued political instability, as well as concern over the disproportionate control of Haitian economic resources by a small number of German colonists present there at the start of the twentieth century.

Apart from helping to train François Duvalier, the USA supported both Duvalier dictatorships financially, to keep Haiti as "a necessary counterpoint to communist Cuba"[10] during the Cold War. Cuba is identified as a training ground for Haitian revolutionaries in *Separation*; indeed Cristobal, the boyfriend of the central female character, Luisa, goes there to study, "to teach [in Haiti] what he has learned [in Cuba]" (55).

The Duvaliers essentially ran fascist regimes based upon violent suppression of all opposition, using their own paramilitary police, the *Tontons Macoutes*, to carry out state violence, central to Luisa's fate in *Separation*. The unnamed fortress prison in the story may be the notorious Fort Dimanche.

The US Carter-led administration (1977-81) placed more emphasis on human rights and gave confidence to Haitian

---

10 — See: Laurent Dubois, 'How Will Haiti Reckon with the Duvalier Years' in *The New Yorker*, 6th October, 2014.

opposition movements. At the time of writing in the late 1970s, Anna Seghers would be reading about rising protest in Haiti,[11] which finally in 1986 forced Bébé Doc into exile, to France, where he remained for twenty-five years. Seghers's prediction of an end to his dictatorship was not unfounded.

Separation takes us beyond the pivotal events of the Haitian Revolution to present-day Haiti of the late 1970s. The euphoric scenes of liberation from a totalitarian regime are measured by caution and uncertainty over the future direction of the country, emphasizing the harsh reality of the Haitian Revolution as a "narrative of liberation that is not yet complete in Haiti's own territory".[12] Indeed, Haiti is a post-colonial state still locked in a decolonizing process[13] several centuries after liberation. Since the downfall of the Duvalier regimes, successive military coups by former regime members have followed. The rule of the first democratically elected Haitian leader, Jean-Bertrand Aristide (1991), ended less than a year later in further military coups. Continued political instability combined with massive debt burden created under the Duvaliers continues to hamper Haiti and its people. As a result, the 2010 earthquake had far more devastating consequences for this, the poorest nation in the Americas.

Examining the Haitian Revolution, its causes and its

---

11 — Seghers intimates her awareness of current events in Haiti in a letter to Haitian economist Pierre-Charles Gérard in December 1978. Characteristically, Seghers also "gathered relevant material, particularly about present-day Haiti and its recent past under 'Papa Doc' and 'Baby Doc' Duvalier" (Christiane Zehl Romero, *Anna Seghers: Eine Biographie 1947-1983*, (Aufbau, 2003), p. 320 [translation D.I.]).

12 — Joseph, 2012, p. 51.

13 — "Decolonization demands a sustained, quotidian commitment to the struggle for national liberation" (Homi Bhaba, 'Foreword: Framing Fanon' in Frantz Fanon, *The Wretched of the Earth*, trans. by Richard Philcox (New York: Grove Press, 2004), p. xvii).

aftermath, helps us to understand the roots of Haitian society with its strong African connections through slavery. *Separation* touches on the importance of Vodou, a "syncretic fusion of African and Christian beliefs"[14] which has deep associations with slavery in Haiti, when it "mimicked and subverted colonial authority".[15] Vodou was also used to radicalize enslaved Haitians to initiate events that lead to the Haitian Revolution.[16] The characters in *Separation* discuss Bébé Doc's misappropriation of Vodou when waiter Juan explains to Luisa that "When we were slaves, Vodou meant something else to us entirely" (59). Bébé Doc used Vodou to justify persecution of Haitian Christians, as alluded to in *Separation* (59), and this misuse of Vodou under the Duvalier regime means that today for Haitian people it represents equally freedom and oppression. Vodou has always been connected with Haitian politics, and it also has cultural associations with the Creole language (itself a fusion of French and African languages), and is integral to Haitian identity today.[17]

14 — Madelaine Hron, *Translating Pain: Immigrant Suffering in Literature and Culture* (Toronto: University of Toronto Press, 2009) p. 140.

15 — Hron, p. 140.

16 — "With otherworldly strength, the legend goes, the world's richest colony was overthrown and the first black republic proclaimed. Haitian Vodou became a religion with rebellion and freedom at its heart." See: https://www.theguardian.com/world/2015/nov/07/vodou-haiti-endangered-faith-soul-of-haitian-people (by Kim Wall and Caterina Clerici).

17 — Anthropologist Ira Lowenthal suggests the Vodou religion in modern-day Haiti is "the soul of Haitian people" in: https://www.theguardian.com/world/2015/nov/07/vodou-haiti-endangered-faith-soul-of-haitian-people (by Kim Wall and Caterina Clerici).

Contributors

Anna Seghers was born to Jewish parents in Mainz, Germany, in 1900, and died in East Berlin in 1983. She won the prestigious Kleist Prize for her debut work, The Revolt of the Fishermen of St. Barbara (1928) and received the Georg Büchner Prize in 1947 for services to German literature, primarily in recognition of her internationally bestselling novel of German pre-war antifascist resistance, The Seventh Cross (1942). During her exile period from Hitler's Germany (1933—1947), she wrote two other enduring works, Transit (1944) and The Excursion of the Dead Girls (1943/4). These three works have recently been freshly translated into English.

Seghers's work from her later period, as a citizen of East Germany, remains largely overlooked in English translation. *Crossing: A Love Story* (1971) was published in 2016 to critical acclaim. *Three Women from Haiti* (1980) is the last story published by this influential German writer.

Recent Seghers English-language translations include *Transit* (New York Review of Books); *The Seventh Cross* (New York Review of Books; Virago Modern Classics); *The Excursion of the Dead Girls, Post to the Promised Land, The End* in *American Imago*, Volume 74, Number 3, Fall 2017, and *Crossing: A Love Story,* also translated by Douglas Irving and published by Diálogos.

Douglas Irving was born in 1972 in Scotland, UK. In the 1990s he studied Spanish and German language and literature at Aberdeen University. In 2013/4 he studied a Masters in

Translation Studies at Glasgow University.

Douglas published his first full translation in 2016, *Crossing: A Love Story*, a late work by the great twentieth-century writer, Anna Seghers. It was instantly hailed as a modern classic. *Three Women from Haiti* is his second translation to be published with Lavender Ink/ Diálogos Books.

In 2019, Douglas's third translation, *Distant Signs*, the debut novel by the German writer and poet Anne Richter, was published by Neem Tree Press.

Marike Janzen is Associate Professor of Humanities at the University of Kansas, and holds a PhD in Comparative Literature from the University of Texas. Her publications on Anna Seghers include the book *Writing to Change the World: Anna Seghers, Authorship, and International Solidarity in the Twentieth Century* (Camden House, 2018), as well as the essay "Between the Pedagogical and the Performative: Personal Stories, Public Narratives, and Social Critique in Anna Seghers's *Überfahrt*" (*German Quarterly*, 2006). Janzen is also the author of numerous articles that explore topics such as the intersection of narrative and rights in Bertolt Brecht and Lynn Nottage, performances of tolerance in the contemporary German literary sphere, and service-learning pedagogy. She is currently at work on a book that examines the way literary texts and institutions respond to the large-scale presence of international refugees in Germany.

https://boydellandbrewer.com/writing-to-change-the-world.html

CPSIA information can be obtained
at www.ICGtesting.com
Printed in the USA
FSHW022055171019